Illustration by
Hiromu Arakawa

FULLMETAL ALCHEMIST

Under the Faraway Sky

Under the Faraway Sky

MAKOTO INOUE

Original Concept by
HIROMU ARAKAWA

Translated by
Alexander O. Smith
with Rich Amtower

VIZ Media
San Francisco

FULLMETAL ALCHEMIST
UNDER THE FARAWAY SKY
© 2004 Hiromu Arakawa, Makoto Inoue/SQUARE ENIX.
First published in Japan in 2004 by SQUARE ENIX CO., LTD.
English translation rights arranged with SQUARE ENIX CO.,
LTD. and VIZ Media, LLC.

Illustrations by Hiromu Arakawa
Cover design by Amy Martin
All rights reserved.

Published by
VIZ Media, LLC
295 Bay Street
San Francisco, CA 94133

www.viz.com

Printed in the U.S.A.

First printing, October 2007

Contents

Under the Faraway Sky

Story One

Under the Faraway Sky

EDWARD DREAMED he was home again.

Familiar sights surrounded him: The hill covered with swaying green grass. Sheep clustered in bunches, grazing. And in the middle of the sheep with their soft, white wool, a shepherd playing the flute. Farmers swinging their hoes, tilling the fields. Old women picking fruit in the orchards. Children racing each other home from school, a gang of dogs yapping and parking at their heels.

One of the dogs broke away from the pack, running up the hill to where Edward stood and sniffing at his feet.

. . . *Den.*

The dog rubbed his leg. Edward gave it a pat on the head. *Winry's dog.* He was a perfect black except for his nose, belly, and the tips at his feet, which were all untarnished white. Edward had helped raise him since he was a pup. Hand resting on the dog's warm head, Edward turned back to the view.

9

Resembool . . .

Edward squinted his eyes as he looked out across the town. The wind, the sky, the trees, the people—all was gentle and calm.

Here, there was none of the refinement of the city. News from the outside world traveled slowly if at all, and every day passed without incident. You could walk down the street alone, and sooner or later, a grown-up would say hi, or a kid your age would invite you to join in on a game. It was a warm town, where people cared for each other.

Edward spotted a boy running down the road and called out to him.

Except he had no voice.

Huh? Why can't I speak?

Forgetting for a moment he was dreaming, Edward went to rub his throat when he realized he was holding a torch in his right hand. His hand, firmly grasping the torch, was of shiny Auto-Mail. Below it, his Auto-Mail left leg shone dully in the torch's reflected light. Edward knew what he had to do.

I have to get out of here. I can't sit here looking at this village. I've made up my mind.

Beneath the blue sky, Resembool looked as peaceful as always. He turned around to see his childhood home, the house where he and his brother had grown up. There were the perennials his mom had planted, growing by the front door. On the wall to the side, he saw footprints left from a jumping contest with a friend years ago. A little tin horse lay on its side in the living room. It had been one of the first things he and Al had made with their alchemy. The scribbling on the edge of the kitchen table, however, was young Winry's work.

Edward set fire to them all and watched the house burn.

The fire was hungry. It consumed everything: the picture books he had read over and over again, photographs still in their frames, the wooden swings in the garden—all his memories, burning.

Edward muttered to himself, the heat of the flames on his face. *"No going back."*

In the dream, Edward heard himself speak. His eyes opened.

BRIGHT SUNLIGHT streamed onto his face. "Nnngh . . ." Edward squinted and sat up.

The afternoon sun spilled in through the window by the bed. Edward reached out his arm to shut the curtain. He poured a cup of water from a flask on the small bedside table and took a swig. "I'm wiped out," he said to no one, falling back onto sheets damp with sweat.

With the curtain closed, the room was dim and growing cooler, which only made Edward's cheek feel hotter. Blond hair stuck to his sweaty forehead. Edward rolled over, wiping golden strands away with his hand.

He knew his weariness and the heat he felt trapped in his body wasn't on account of the sun.

"Unnnh . . ." Edward groaned, coughed twice into his hand, and glared at the ceiling. Several days before, Edward had been out in the rain and caught a cold.

If his brother, Alphonse, hadn't noticed he was running a temperature the night before and arranged for their stay in this village, he would probably be out lying by the side of some road somewhere dying. At least that's how it felt to Edward.

Luckily, Alphonse had found someone who could offer them a place to stay—an empty house whose owner was out of town for a while—and procured blankets and a bed. As soon as the bed was made, he had pushed Edward into it despite his brother's protestations.

"You've been running yourself ragged, and now it's caught up to you," he had said. "You'd better rest now, or all those corners you've been cutting to get this far will come back and take their revenge!"

"Exhausted . . . " Edward looked back up at the ceiling. He was alone, with only a small kitchen, the bed, a table, and a chair to keep him company while Alphonse went out looking for a doctor.

A breeze ruffled the curtains and brushed across his cheek.

"It's been almost a year," Edward whispered suddenly. It had been a year since they had left Resembool. Of course he was exhausted, and dreaming of home.

When they had left, he had been twelve. Now Edward was thirteen. His blond hair, braided in the back, had grown longer, and his golden eyes had a world-weary look to them. Still, no matter how much he had changed inside, on the outside he was still a boy, and the endless hard trekking across the countryside took its toll—both mental and physical.

Yet he had to keep going. He had to get his and Alphonse's bodies back.

Their intent hadn't been evil, that was certain, but they had broken one of the most sacred alchemical taboos. They had thought human transmutation was the only way they could see their mother again after her death. But, right or wrong, the alchemy had failed. The brothers didn't get their mother back, and in exchange for their foolishness, Edward lost his left leg and Alphonse, his entire body. Fearing he would lose the only family he had left, Edward performed one more act of alchemy. Though it cost him his right arm, he managed at last to attach his brother's soul to a suit of armor.

Now, Edward's right arm and left leg were no longer flesh but Auto-Mail, and Alphonse was a voice and a personality attached to a giant suit of bronze armor so large and menacing that it was hard to believe he was the younger of the two by a year.

Many people would have considered themselves lucky and called it quits there, but not Edward and Alphonse. They wanted their old bodies back.

Edward became a state alchemist. The funding he would have at his disposal and his newfound access to information would make it easier to track down a way they might recover their bodies. What did it matter if people called him the army's lapdog? Alphonse joined him, and they had never looked back.

But their year on the road had been tough. Out here, weariness built up in hours and days. Edward's body had been waiting for an excuse to give out.

"No way am I sleeping away the whole day here," Edward muttered, trying to sit up again. His limbs felt like they were made of concrete.

"Darn it, time's a-wasting!" Edward snapped, angry at his body's betrayal. How could he be forced to sit in one place now, when his objective was so clear? Edward angrily kicked the covers off the bed.

"Hey, I thought I told you to take it easy," Alphonse cried. He had only just opened the door and spied his brother moaning on the bed, the covers in loose piles on the floor. "Your blanket fell off." He picked up the blankets and tucked his brother back in, seeming for all the world like the older of the two. His armor suit was scary to behold, but the personality it held was that of a caring, gentle-natured boy.

Edward, on the other hand, was a fighter. He preferred moving and acting to sitting and thinking. Just like when he became a state alchemist at an unprecedented young age, once he decided something, he moved.

"Al, let's get out of here."

"Huh?"

"Look, I'm fine. I want to get over those mountains and into a larger town. Maybe we'll find a lead on the Philosopher's Stone."

The Philosopher's Stone—this legendary artifact, fabled to possess the power to amplify the effects of alchemy—had been the sole focus of their wanderings. Without something that could circumvent the fundamental law of alchemy—the conservation of mass known as equivalent exchange—human transmutation was impossible. If anything held the key to breaking that law, it was the Philosopher's Stone that would make it possible.

But the stone, their one hope in the world, was little more than a myth. No one alive had ever held it. Its very existence was uncertain. It wasn't easy finding clues, either. Edward and Alphonse had ridden train after train, visiting large towns, occasionally tromping across mountains into the wilderness, looking for any scrap of information about the stone's where-abouts or method of manufacture that they could find. But they had made a decision to not stop until they had searched right up to the ends of the earth, and so they had to keep moving. Any untrodden land, any unvisited town held potential . . . but Alphonse wouldn't let Edward out of bed.

"You've still got a fever. We can't leave now." Alphonse poured the rest of the water in the flask into a wash basin and soaked the towel hanging on its edge. "I found a doctor and asked him to visit. You sleep till he comes, 'kay?"

"You . . . found a doctor?" Edward made a sour face. Edward had been sure Alphonse's search for a hospital would be in vain this far from a big city. In fact, he had been counting on it. If a doctor came to check him, there would be no way to hide his fever. He might really be forced to sit here until it broke, and that could take days. For Edward, who wanted only to leave as soon as possible, a doctor was his worst fear.

Alphonse could see right through him. "You're getting a checkup, and that's that. I've never seen you with a fever this high. I've been worried. I mean, what if you're really sick?"

Edward frowned and fell silent, suddenly feeling guilty for making his brother worry. Alphonse gently placed the wet towel on his forehead. "When I described your symptoms to the doctor, he said it was probably just a cold, but you should wait till you're better before leaving again. I think we got lucky, really. I wasn't sure I'd be able to find anyone out here. Apparently, he's the only doctor in the area—he was so busy, he couldn't come himself, but he said he'd send his assistant along with some medicine."

"Great," Edward replied, seeing potential for compromise. "Then, once I've got my checkup and medicine, let's head out. Fine?"

"Not fine. Not a chance!"

"But I can't lie around here sleeping!" Edward kicked off the covers once again. "I'll sleep on the train! What if some clue slips away while we're here, loafing around?! See? I'm fine, really!"

"Your mouth is fine, sure. I'm not so sure about the rest of you."

"It's just a little fever," Edward said, starting to sit up. "I mean . . . nngh!"

Alphonse jabbed a thermometer under his tongue. "Sit still. The doctor wanted me to take your temperature. And this isn't our thermometer, so don't break it."

On any other day, Edward would have been quick enough to dodge the thermometer, but his fever had slowed him down considerably. Alphonse was forcing him back down onto the bed when they heard a young man's voice calling from outside.

"Here for the checkup! Is this where the patient is?"

"Sounds like the assistant's come."

Alphonse stood up immediately. Behind him, Edward muttered under his breath "Great. I'll just pretend I'm better for the doc, and we can skedaddle out of here . . ." He was grateful for Alphonse's concern, but he had more important things to do than "take it easy."

Edward pulled the thermometer out of his mouth and glanced at it. *Ninety-nine already.* If he left it in there, it would go over one hundred for sure. Edward quickly sloshed the remaining water from his cup into his mouth, and slipped the thermometer back below his tongue.

Ninety-nine is good. Don't want it to be too low or they'll suspect something. Edward grinned just as Alphonse turned. "Hey, what's the thermometer . . ."

"Take a look." Edward casually took the thermometer out of his mouth, and put it on the table.

17

"Good timing. We can show it to the doctor now." Alphonse turned back around to the door. "If he's actually coming." He cupped a hand to his mouth and called out the door, "Are you still there?"

"Sorry! Coming in now! Sorry to keep you . . . urk?"

Alphonse staggered back, his mind processing several things at once. First, the doctor had been an older, gentle fellow with a warm demeanor, and he had expected something similar from his assistant. It was clear from the assistant's voice that he was much younger. Alphonse just hadn't expected someone so young . . . or so familiar looking.

The boy who stood in their doorway wore glasses on his freckled face and carried a bag of doctor's instruments under his arm. His hair was short and wavy brown, and his eyes were a rusty green. He wore cream-colored knee-length pants, and his skinny arms protruded from a black shirt. He looked like a boy who had just been out playing in the mountains.

The boy looked up at Alphonse in shock—though his expression wasn't the usual surprise at seeing a walking, talking suit of armor. Alphonse, too, stood speechless.

"Is something wrong?" Edward called out from his bed, seeing Alphonse frozen by the door. Then he looked past him and yelped.

The three boys' eyes met, and after a pause, they all shouted at once.

"Pitt!"

"Edward and Alphonse!"

"It is you, isn't it!"

Pitt Renbak was the Elric brothers' friend from Resembool. He had never worn glasses, but his fearless smile and eyes were exactly the same as they remembered.

"Wow! Long time, no see! What are you doing out here?" Pitt asked with a smile as he ran to Edward's bedside.

"I was just about to ask you!" Edward said, ignoring his body's protests as he sat up and got out of bed.

Back in Resembool, Edward and Pitt had been inseparable. No matter what was up, one was always with the other, and hardly a day passed when they didn't talk. There were similarities beyond their shared hometown. Edward had lost his father when he was young, and Pitt's father was gone most of the year for his work. The only difference was that Pitt admired his father, a traveling physician, while Edward hated his.

Lack of a father had made them similar in another way too: both boys had grown up in part supporting their mothers, which give them independence and courage beyond that of their peers. Pitt and Edward were the natural leaders of the town children. Yet, all the same, they were still boys. Independence and courage easily turned into headstrong recklessness, and the two had hurt themselves badly time and again, making secret forts in trees or getting stuck in muddy streams. In the end, they generally provided their mothers with more trouble than help.

"When was the last time I saw you? Has it already been a year?"

"Since we left Resembool, I guess."

"I was wondering what happened to you."

"Same here."

Edward and Pitt grinned and faced one another.

"Really . . ."

Suddenly, the boys' hands shot into the air. Each put their fingers together, making a flat surface with their palms, and lowered their hands slowly until each rested on the other's head. The two boys' eyes opened wide.

"I won!" they shouted at the same time, then a second later, glared at each other.

"No way! I totally won. I'm way taller than you."

"Excuse me? What are you talking about? I'm clearly taller."

Edward took his hand away from Pitt's forehead, brought it to his own head, and slid it back. His hand passed over Pitt's head without even touching his hair. "See? Way taller. Phew. And here I'd spent the whole year worrying about it."

With a flourish Edward lowered his hand.

Now Pitt's hand shot through the air, clearing Edward's head. "See that? Proof. Don't try to fool me."

"Eh? Right. You stood on your toes. Why don't you just admit the truth: you're shorter than I am."

"Why don't *you* just admit the fact that you're the village runt?"

Alphonse sighed as the two of them took turns swiping their hands over each other's head. Edward had clearly forgotten about his fever, and Pitt had completely forgotten that he'd come to check on Edward's health.

"Some things never change," Alphonse sighed.

As they had found out on many occasions, being similar didn't necessarily mean that Edward and Pitt always got along. Because they were always the top two kids in the village, they constantly competed for the number-one spot. Test scores, track time, arm wrestling, even how fast they could eat their food . . . everything was an open competition, and never more so than when the subject of their height was on the line. The two had squared off for as long as Alphonse could remember, and a satisfactory conclusion had never been reached.

"Look, it's a fact. You're shorter than I am."

"Look who's talking! And it just so happens, I'm in the middle of a growth spurt right now. I've been shooting up for the last year."

"You've had a growth spurt? *I've* had a growth spurt! I'm taller. Look, if you won't take my word for it, let's ask Alphonse."

"Okay, Al, measure time!"

Edward and Pitt stood back-to-back. Alphonse shook his head gravely. "I've measured you two a hundred times. It's no good. You won't believe me."

No matter how scientifically accurate his measurements were, if Alphonse said Edward were taller, Pitt would be furious, and if he said Pitt were taller, Edward would make him do it again. Alphonse shrugged and picked Pitt's bag up from the floor. A stethoscope and other doctor's instruments peeked out of the open bag top.

"Is measuring your height really that important right now?" Alphonse asked their old friend.

"I'm surprised you're a doctor's assistant already, Pitt. Er, you came here to check up on my brother right? Maybe you should just go ahead and have a look . . ."

"Is it really important!" The two glared at Alphonse, scowls on their faces. "Of course it's important! Isn't it, Pitt?"

"You know it, Edward!"

"Now they agree," Alphonse said, shaking his head and wondering how to break the stalemate.

Pitt suddenly pulled his back away from Edward. "Fine, fine."

Setting his glasses straight on his nose, Pitt opened his bag, took out his instruments, and pushed Edward back onto the bed. "Okay, checkup time. Open up."

Suddenly the doctor's assistant again, Pitt pulled out a wooden tongue depressor and a small mirror on an extender and knelt down beside the bed.

"Look who's the professional now. You're really working at that clinic? I figured you'd still be bossing around the kids back in Resembool . . . ngak!"

Pitt thrust the tongue depressor mercilessly into Edward's mouth.

"Likewise. Here I was, thinking everything was business as usual when I hear you'd run off after becoming a state alchemist.

I figured you'd gotten sick of the army already and headed home. Didn't expect to find you out here catching colds."

Edward's pithy comeback was lost in a loud gagging as Pitt gleefully jammed more instruments into his mouth.

Edward's Auto-Mail surgery and rehabilitation had happened back at home, so people from Resembool knew about his arm and leg and Alphonse's suit of armor. But no one knew the real reason for their accident, and no one knew that there wasn't any Alphonse inside that suit. Some might've had inklings of the truth, but no one pressed for details, and Edward and his brother had never openly discussed the matter.

Even their young friend Pitt realized that some things were better left unasked, and although he had visited Edward frequently during his recovery, Pitt had never probed deeper. Nor did he ever learn the real reason why Edward had gone off to become a state alchemist at such a young age.

"Oooh, your throat's pretty swollen. I'm surprised you're even able to eat," Pitt said, jerking the tongue depressor around in Edward's mouth violently as he peered down his throat. Edward protested. "Eeeh! An't ou o hat any entler?!"

"I'm afraid this is as gentle as it gets. Okay, back next! Gotta listen to your lungs."

Edward felt rough hands grab his shoulders and flip him over. A metal stethoscope pressed against his back.

"Hey! That's cold! So . . . why are you a doctor's assistant out here anyway? Wait, your dad didn't open up a clinic in this town, did he?"

"My dad, settle down? Not a chance. He's still wandering the countryside, as always."

"So you came here to study by yourself? Wow, Pitt," said Alphonse, sounding honestly impressed. "And they're trusting you to make house calls already. Pretty impressive, huh, Edward?"

Edward had trouble sharing his younger brother's enthusiasm. Pitt, like him, was only thirteen years old. But now Edward was a state alchemist, and Pitt was out here learning a trade. Even their friend Winry was an Auto-Mail technician in training, helping Pinako back home. Edward couldn't shake the feeling that they were all a bit young to be so . . . so responsible.

"You're still thirteen, right?" Edward said with a wry smile. "I mean, I feel a little nervous letting you check me out."

Edward and Pitt had been fighting since before they could even talk. When Edward thought of Pitt, he pictured the wild boy running down the street, not the stethoscope-wearing apprentice physician standing in front of them. When Pitt grabbed his shoulder a few moments before, he had been half afraid that his old friend was going to take advantage of his fever to get him in a wrestling lock.

"Actually . . . I'm fourteen," came his friend's voice from above him. He heard Pitt snort triumphantly. "Birthday was last week."

Even though he was facing downward, Edward had no

trouble imagining Pitt's smile. "Darn! I can't believe it's that time of year already . . ."

The two delighted in competing at everything, but the one thing in which there was no contest was their ages. Even though they were only apart by a few months, for those few months after Pitt's birthday and before his, Edward was a year younger, and Pitt loved nothing more than to rub it in. It was tradition. Edward half hoped that Pitt had forgotten after they'd missed each other's birthdays the year before.

No such luck.

Edward looked up. Pitt was grinning down at him. "Grow up, would ya?" he said, like he had said every year Edward could remember.

Edward gnashed his teeth together and was about to say something when Alphonse cut him off.

"Say, Pitt, how long do you think it will take my brother to recover?"

Pitt removed the stethoscope from his ears. "Well, he should really stay in bed for another two days. This cold's been going around, and it has a way of coming back when you least expect it."

"What?!" Edward protested loudly. "Two more days? No! Look, I'm better already."

Even though his arms felt heavy, Edward refused to show any sign of weakness. Truth be told, seeing his old friend had picked up his spirits considerably. Hopefully, Edward thought,

Pitt would mistake that for an improvement in his health. *After all, he's only an assistant doctor. I can fool him!* Edward sat up in bed, swinging his arms around to show how good he was feeling. "See? I'm ready to leave right now!"

"I can't believe you're still saying that," Alphonse said with a entreating look at Pitt. "What do you think?"

"What was your temperature?" their friend asked, reaching out a hand toward Edward as he cleaned up his instruments. "You took your temperature, right? If it was under a hundred, fine, you can leave."

"Well would you look at that!" Edward said, triumphantly brandishing the thermometer and placing it in Pitt's hand. "Ninety-nine on the dot! Thanks, Doc!"

Pitt finished packing his small bag and stared at the thermometer with a steady eye before placing it on the table. Then he sighed.

"What? Ack!"

Pitt slapped a hand across Edward's forehead, pushing him back down into the bed.

"Hey, what's the big idea?"

"You do have a fever. You can fool the thermometer, but you can't fool me! Aha!" Pitt picked up the cup from the bedside table. Only a few drops of water remained in the bottom. "You put water in your mouth!"

Pitt slammed the cup down on the desk. A few droplets of water jumped out onto Edward's indignant scowl. He wiped them off. "Oh, yeah? You have proof? Show me proof!"

"There was water on the thermometer! And you were the one who taught me this trick in the first place, Ed!"

"Oh . . . Did I?" Now that he mentioned it, it did sound like the kind of discovery he'd have shared with Pitt back in the day.

Pitt put away the thermometer and thrust an accusing finger at his friend. "I know all your tricks, buddy. Listen, come to the clinic tomorrow and have the doctor give you a look-over. You're not leaving this village until you're better."

Edward didn't take well to orders. "Says who? What gives you the authority?!"

"I'm your doctor. The first person who saw you here was me. That makes me your primary-care physician. I'm the one responsible for keeping you healthy," Pitt proclaimed, setting a packet of medicine down on the bedside table. "Drink this, and stay in bed. This cold can be rough. A lot of people in town have been laid up in bed with it. In fact, I recommend that once your fever goes down, you go back to Resembool a while for some rest."

"I'm not going home over a cold."

Pitt smiled at his friend. "It won't be that bad. Why, you could have Winry look after you."

Winry was an Auto-Mail technician in training, the grand-daughter of famed Auto-Mail technician Pinako Rockbell, who had crafted both Edward's arm and leg. Edward and Winry had hung out a lot when they were kids, because their parents had been friends, and Pitt always liked to make fun of them.

"Have her take care of me? She'll take care of me all right. I'd never walk again!"

"Oh, did I touch a sore spot?"

"Grrr . . . !"

Before Edward, growling at him from the bed, could pounce, Pitt picked up his doctor's bag and turned toward the door. "Later!"

"Oh . . . thanks!" Alphonse said, following him to the door. "I've never seen him with a fever that high. I was really worried. Thanks for coming to check on him."

Behind his brother, Edward glowered daggers at Pitt. Pitt glanced back at him and gave Alphonse a slap on the shoulder. "I'm afraid there's no cure for your brother," he whispered.

"What? What do you mean?" For a moment, Alphonse was afraid that their friend had seen something worse than just a cold when he looked in Edward's mouth.

Pitt nodded gravely. "See, the problem is, I don't have any medicine for idiocy."

"I heard that!" Edward cried, making to leap out of bed, but Pitt stuck out his tongue and sped off.

"Wait up!"

"Ed!" Alphonse grabbed Edward by the collar as he made for the door and dragged him back to bed. "You have to get your rest!"

Edward slumped back into the bed, the fight gone out of him. "I feel worse than I did when he got here."

"It's your own fault for running around. Your fever will

just get worse!" Edward spread out the blanket bunched up by his brother's feet, and tucked him in. "What a surprise. I never expected to run into our old friends out here. Pitt's as sour-mouthed as ever, but I think he gave you a good checkup. He seems more mature now. So stop playing pranks and help him help you get better, okay?"

"Bah." Edward frowned, wiping the sweat off his forehead, and stared up at the ceiling. "Surprising that he wants to be a doctor."

Pitt's father wasn't a surgeon or one of those kind of doctors. Rather, he traveled the land, gathering information about medicinal herbs, searching for new plants in the hinterlands, and handing out medicine in towns that didn't have a doctor of their own. Edward had never seen him personally, but he knew that people back home respected him greatly.

He also knew that Pitt respected him too, but he'd never heard him say he wanted to be a doctor. Yet, here he was, well on the way to becoming one.

Edward tried to match the Pitt he had just seen with the year-old image in his head and soon gave up. Edward felt the passing of time more than ever. "I suppose things are bound to change when you're away so long."

Edward put his arm over his forehead and closed his eyes.

Alphonse was right—his fever had gone up. He could feel the heat trapped inside his body. Only the Auto-Mail against his forehead was cool.

That alone hadn't changed.

IT WAS ALREADY LATE morning when Edward jumped out of bed. He had made up his mind to go to the clinic, if only to avert Pitt's wrath. Though it ate at him to admit it, his friend was right. His fever had gone down a lot thanks to the medicine, and he figured that the quickest way out of this was to go to the clinic, get some stronger medicine, and get well as soon as possible.

As he opened the door, the sunlight reflecting off a nearby river caught his eye. Their borrowed house bordered a field some distance away from town, with a view over sloping pastures dotted with humble homes, a single large river running through the middle.

Edward looked around to find Alphonse by the side of the house, washing his clothes for him.

"Hey, Al, I'm off to the clinic. Which way is it?"

Alphonse turned to look at him, his hands still in the bucket of soapy water. "Huh? Didn't Pitt say for you to drop in after lunch?"

"Look, I'm not waiting around in this town any longer than I have to . . . and, gee, you didn't have to wash my clothes for me, Al . . ."

Alphonse laughed brightly. "The doc said you need your rest, and I don't want you out here getting all wet and catching another cold." Alphonse stood, hung his brother's clothes on pegs set under the eaves of the house, and joined Edward. "The clinic's thataway. Just across the river," he said, pointing down a narrow path that ran between two plots of pasture.

The two walked down the path, glancing at the few houses they could see in the distance.

"Pretty rural, huh?" It had been night when they first arrived, and with his high fever, Edward hadn't taken proper stock of their surroundings. A look at the abandoned farmhouses here and there and the generous amounts of pasture land offered all the proof he needed that they were officially in the countryside.

"This used to be a booming place with a productive coal mine, but it's been closed for some time now," Alphonse said, pointing off toward some low rocky hills to the side of the village. Edward spotted a cavelike opening in the hills—most likely the entrance to the mines. Even from this distance, he could clearly see the boards blocking the mouth of the mine. From the look of it, they had been there for quite some time. Grass grew thick over the boards and the walls of the mine entrance.

Apparently, the local economy had shifted to agriculture. The few people they saw were out working in their fields, cutting hay, or tending sheep. One farmer stood up as they passed, noticing Alphonse, and waved to them. "Ahoy, there! Off to the clinic?"

"Ah, that's the fellow who's lending us our house." Alphonse waved back. "Hello! We might have to borrow the house a little longer. I hope that's all right?"

"Oh, fine by me. The owner's off living with relatives in another town to find work. Won't be back for some time."

"Thank you!"

"Rest well, now!"

"Thanks!"

The man waved again, then went back to swinging his hoe.

"People have been moving away from the countryside here—and not just miners, either. There's only the one doctor." Alphonse said, looking across the river to the far bank. "The clinic here is the last in the area."

They came to a place where a bridge crossed the slow-flowing river. On the other side, they saw a low wooden structure. This was the clinic where Pitt worked.

"That the place? Surprising that Pitt would come all the way out here to become an apprentice . . ."

"Yeah, I know. I wonder how long he's been at it."

"Well, he didn't say anything when we last saw him a year ago. Maybe this is a recent development for him?"

Edward stepped onto the bridge. A breeze coming across the pastures ruffled his hair. "What are you going to do while I'm getting my checkup, Al?"

"Oh, I'll just wait here until you're done," his brother replied, attempting—poorly—to hide the concern in his voice.

Edward shrugged. "My fever's down. I'll be fine. And you've been watching over me all this time. You should go take a look around. If this is the only clinic, there's no telling how crowded it will be. I could be a while."

Alphonse's lack of a real body meant he could never tire, but he could still get bored, and looking after his sick brother couldn't have been all that exciting.

"Okay, well, if you take too long, I'll just head home myself. No lying to the doctor and saying you're feeling better when you aren't, now!"

"Would I do a thing like that?"

"You did yesterday! Why do you think I've been watching over you like a hawk?" Alphonse replied with a laugh.

Edward grinned and rapped him on the shoulder with an Auto-Mail fist. He knew his brother teased him to hide how worried he was, and Edward appreciated it. He waved and then turned toward the clinic.

IN FRONT of the small building hung a sign that read "Dr. Norm's Health Clinic." A small garden grew there, where bushes and flowering plants Edward had never seen swayed gently in the breeze. From the slight medicinal smell that drifted on the wind, he surmised they were herbs and strongly scented flowers, the kind used to make potpourri. Edward gave a sidelong glance at the patch as he opened the double doors to the clinic.

He had expected it to be crowded, but only five people were sitting on the bench in the waiting room when he walked in. One had bandages on his arm, but all the others were coughing, and their faces looked feverish—victims of the same cold that Edward had caught. Edward cut across the waiting room, stopping before the counter at the front.

The space behind the counter served as both reception

desk and apothecary. It was cluttered with various bottles, all filled with strange powders and liquids. Behind it stood Pitt. He paced around busily, a pharmaceutical guide in hand, opening bottles to take out medicine, measuring small piles of powder on a scale, checking a list of ingredients, and stuffing the finished product into a bag.

Pitt carried the bag out through the door next to the counter into the waiting room, where he handed it to a young woman who looked dressed for the road.

She probably came from a nearby village, thought Edward.

"Your symptoms haven't changed from last week, so I've given you another week's worth of the same medicine. Come back next week, and the doctor will see how you're doing."

Edward sat in stunned silence. He couldn't believe his ears. The only one in Resembool with a fouler mouth and quicker temper than Edward was Pitt, and here he was, being *polite.* His friend glanced to the side and noticed Edward, sitting with his mouth open. "Oh, it's you. Didn't I tell you to come in the afternoon?"

"When did you get all polite?!"

"Huh? Oh, that . . ." For a moment, Pitt looked embarrassed, but soon remembered himself and returned Edward's glare. "What about you, army man? Didn't they drill any manners into you?"

"Me?" Edward shook his head. "Never."

Edward couldn't recall minding his words once, whether he was speaking to a superior or hanging out in the barracks.

"You serious? What ever happened to military polish?" Pitt stared at Edward a moment longer before returning behind his counter. "Though . . . I guess it is *you* we're talking about."

"What's that supposed to mean?" Edward growled, knowing exactly what it was supposed to mean.

"Doc's out making house calls. He should be back soon. Why don't you sit and wait," Pitt suggested, turning back to the phials of medicine. He carefully poured powder from one into a bowl and began to grind the powder with a small stick.

Apparently, the people in the waiting room were waiting not for a checkup but for medicine. Pitt prepared their prescriptions one at a time, carefully explaining what was inside each packet to each patient. He spoke loudly to an elderly man who was hard of hearing, and held the door for a mother carrying a small child.

Edward stared from the bench at Pitt's almost gentlemanly manner. It was a side of his friend he had never seen in Resembool. "Wow," he muttered under his breath. Everyone had received their medicine and left, leaving him alone in the waiting room.

"What's that?" Pitt asked while cleaning up the bottles behind the counter.

"Don't you do any checkups? You came all the way out to see me yesterday. Seems like you could've given those people their checkups now and saved the doctor a bit of work."

"Oh, I don't normally do those. I only went to see you because the doctor was so busy yesterday, and from the symptoms Alphonse described, we were pretty sure it was this bug that's been going around. You still had to come in here for your real checkup, remember?"

"Well, after all that talk about being my primary care physician yesterday . . ."

"To tell the truth, I wish I could be, but . . ." Pitt trailed off mid-sentence.

Edward looked up to see his friend staring at him from behind the counter, a smile playing on his lips. "Anyway, isn't your primary physician Winry? I wouldn't want to step on her turf."

"That's about enough of that!"

"Oh? But I've got so much more where that came from . . ."

Edward shot up, kicking the bench with his heel as he launched toward the counter. Pitt leaned toward him, fists raised, when the door to the clinic banged open. A woman walked in, carrying a boy of about five years in her arms.

"Doctor!"

"Ah, Ms. Rymar . . ." Pitt backed away from the counter, hastily lowering his fists.

"It's Danny—he won't stop coughing! Where's Dr. Norm? Doctor!" the woman shouted, pushing past Edward to run to the counter.

"There's no need to panic, ma'am," Pitt said calmly. "I'm sorry, but the doctor is currently out on a house call."

"Then bring me some of the medicine from before! You still have some back there, don't you?"

"I'm afraid I'm not allowed to fill new prescriptions."

"But my son!"

As if on cue, the young boy in her arms began to cough and moan. Pitt opened the door and led the two into the examination room. "You can rest here on the bed until the doctor comes," Edward heard him say. "I'll boil some water—the steam should help ease his symptoms temporarily."

"I don't want to ease them, I want to stop them!" the mother cried, waving a hand wildly as he spoke. The back of her hand struck the side of Pitt's face, knocking his glasses to the floor. "It's worthless talking to you! Call the doctor now!"

"He should be back anytime now, ma'am. Let's just do what we can until then," Pitt said, keeping his eyes locked on her. He didn't even glance at his fallen glasses. Edward could tell he was choosing his words carefully to avoid further agitating the woman.

"You're just an assistant! What do you know!" she continued relentlessly.

"Well, the doctor told me that steam works best when Danny's symptoms got bad. You know that, Ms. Rymar."

"Of course, of course," she said, frowning. "I just don't feel comfortable without Dr. Norm here!" In her arms, the boy's cough seemed to be getting worse.

"Hey . . ." Edward said in a low voice. "If you want to help out your kid, how about letting the doctor's assistant do his job? If the doctor showed him what to do, what's the problem trusting him to do it?"

Edward and Pitt spent much of their youth glowering at

one another from either side of a pair of raised fists, but when one of them was in trouble, they had a way of helping each other out. Pitt didn't seem to appreciate the gesture this time.

"Quiet, Edward. This doesn't involve you," his friend said sharply.

"Sure, it doesn't involve me," Edward said, surprised at the response. Then he whispered in Pitt's ear, "I was just wondering when you were going to stop taking crap from this lady."

For a moment, Pitt seemed to waver. Then he reached down and picked up his glasses, and glared through them at Edward. "Just leave me alone, okay?"

"Hey, you can do what you like. I'm just worried about the kid," Edward retorted, not very convincingly.

The sound of the clinic door opening broke the tension. "What's all this? Is something the matter?" In came a man in a white physician's smock, a black leather bag in one hand.

"Dr. Norm!" The woman ran over to him. "My son's having another attack!"

"Ah, so that was the coughing I heard. Don't worry, I'll take a look at him right now. Come along inside."

So this is Pitt's mentor, Dr. Norm, thought Edward. The doctor calmly looked at the boy in the woman's arms. He opened the door to the examination room, showing the mother and child inside, then turned back around to smile wryly at Edward and Pitt in the waiting room. "Well now, I don't know what those glances you two were giving each other were about, but I won't have any fighting in here. Pitt, go boil some water . . . and you'd better get more of that medicine from the cabinets in back."

"Uh, yes, Dr. Norm." Pitt retreated toward a door in the back of the examination room, and Dr. Norm smiled gently at Edward. "And you must be Edward. Pitt told me about you. I'll see you as soon as I'm done with Danny here."

A short while later, the mother walked back into the waiting room, her son Danny now walking by her side.

"Take care. The next time he has an attack, try to stay calm and boil some water. Okay?" Dr. Norm opened the door to the clinic and showed the woman out.

"That boy, is he going to be okay?" Edward asked, in the now-silent waiting room. From the child's heavy coughing and the woman's panic, he feared the boy might have a serious condition.

"Oh, it's nothing too bad. He's not sick, per se. He was just born with weak lungs. As long as you stay calm and do the right thing, he's fine, but his mother gets so worried she wants to stuff him full of medicine. Not that I don't understand, but I try to avoid prescribing too much of the stronger kinds . . . " Dr. Norm said with a frown, waving Edward into the examination room. "You're up next. Thanks for waiting."

Inside, Edward saw Pitt picking up a bowl of steaming water from the corner of the room. He shot a look back at his friend, and Pitt returned the glare through steamed glasses.

"Looks like I can't leave you two alone for a moment, can I," Dr. Norm said with a chuckle. He pulled a sheet of paper out of a small desk and handed it to Pitt. "It's going to rain soon, and I want you to fetch the herbs on this list before then."

"Yes, Dr. Norm."

Pitt stood there for a moment, as though he were going to say something, but then thought better of it and left the room. Just before he disappeared through the door, he turned and stuck his tongue out at Edward.

Edward stuck his tongue out back at him, his smile abruptly becoming a look of surprise when Dr. Norm slapped a cold stethoscope on his chest. "Okay, enough funny faces. Now hold your breath. I'm going to listen to your lungs."

Alone with the doctor in the examination room, Edward held his breath and looked at Pitt's new mentor.

Dr. Norm was an older man. He already had several white hairs on his head. He seemed lively enough, though, and he would certainly have to be as the only doctor in these parts.

"Breathe out slowly, there. Once more. I heard you had a fever. How high did it get?"

"It was just over a hundred yesterday. I'm not sure how high it was before we got to town."

"Well, that boy in the armor said that when you came in, you could barely think straight. I wouldn't be surprised if you were over 105. Still, you've made a lot of improvement. Must have a good constitution. Probably don't catch too many colds, am I right?"

"Well, not too often."

"It's good to be healthy," Dr. Norm said, nodding his head and peering inside Edward's mouth. "Ah, yes, this swelling is a fairly common symptom. You still have a fever, too. I'll give you some antibacterial mouthwash. You need to get plenty of rest."

"So . . . I still have to stay in bed?" Edward asked.

"You look like a lad in a hurry to get out of town," Dr. Norm laughed, making the wrinkles at the corners of his eyes deepen into valleys. "I won't hold you against your will, but do yourself a favor and wait until the fever is gone." Dr. Norm smiled gently and began measuring out medicine.

"How long has Pitt been here, anyway?" Edward asked. He had thought his friend's move was a recent thing, but Pitt seemed so different. The boy that had seen Edward and Alphonse off from Resembool had been just a kid. There were still traces of the old Pitt left, to be sure, but he seemed so much more settled now, and seeing him be polite to customers blew Edward's mind. Part of him wondered how Pitt had managed to make it happen.

"Well, let's see, Pitt got here about a year ago," Dr. Norm replied, pouring various substances out of bottles.

"A year ago?" That meant Pitt had left town right after they had.

"He just showed up one day, asking me to make him an apprentice. Sure, I needed the help, but we are so out-of-the-way here. I didn't see the point in him wasting way his youth in the middle of nowhere, so I advised him to head for a larger town with a proper hospital, but he was adamant."

"Why?"

"Apparently, his father is a traveling doctor who specializes in herbal medicine. It tends to be a great deal cheaper than the processed stuff."

"Yeah, I'd heard that."

"Of course, some diseases can't be cured with herbal remedies, but they *are* great for prevention and general wellness. And expensive drugs with nasty side effects are more trouble than they're worth for people short on money or with weak constitutions. Sounds like those are the sorts of people your friend most wants to help. That's why he chose to study out here—we have lots of medicinal herbs here, you see. Before now, we used mostly processed drugs at the clinic, but since Pitt came, our herbal remedies have really grown. It's helped to keep down costs, too."

Edward nodded, processing this new information about his friend.

"Of course, he is just an apprentice, and I try not to ask too much of him. I never let him touch the dangerous stuff or the really strong medicines. He's done well for himself, though. It's not an easy life out here, but he's making the best of it."

Dr. Norm put the medicine in a small bag and turned around, pointing at a bruise on Edward's arm. "Looks like you've been through quite a lot, too. You've got more cuts and scrapes than skin, my boy."

Edward's arms and legs were covered with scratches and bruises—signs of the tough journey.

"Ah, it's nothing. I just leave them, and they get better after a while."

"That's for a doctor to decide, Edward. Let me see now," Dr. Norm demanded gently, but firmly. "Some of these might benefit from a poultice or a little salve."

Edward meekly submitted to an examination, thinking Dr. Norm was awfully nice for an overworked doctor with an entire village to take care of. Even if he weren't the only doctor in town, his warm bedside manner would guarantee his clinic never lacked for patients.

Dr. Norm finished checking all of his scratches and bruises, put on a few bandages, and rubbed on a little salve before grinning at Edward. "You and Pitt are a lot alike."

"Huh?"

"Do you know why you caught this cold?" Edward looked up at the unexpected question and found himself staring into Dr. Norm's gentle eyes.

"You say you're usually healthy, but you've got a cold because you're exhausted. I don't mean you just got tired, I mean your days and days on the road have all added up . . . and wiped you out. You should relax a bit. Take it easy." Dr. Norm gave Edward a light tap on the shoulder.

It was already afternoon when Edward left the clinic. He walked out of the waiting room, filled with people waiting for afternoon checkups, and went outside to find that the weather had turned for the worse as the doctor had warned. The sun that sparkled so brightly on the river that morning now seemed completely shrouded in clouds.

Walking across the bridge, Edward caught the conversation of some local kids playing on the riverbank.

"Looks like it's gonna rain. We should get home."

"Yeah, I didn't bring an umbrella."

"I gotta go to Cassie's house and give her this grasshopper."

"Mom says I can have a donut when I get home!"

"No way, I wish we had donuts!"

The boys clambered up from the riverbank, boxes and nets for catching insects clutched in her hands, and found their way along the path.

Edward stopped at the highest point of the bowlike bridge. From there, he could see the whole town. He stood there a while, watching the boys run off home. They ran straight, without a glance back.

He saw Pitt in the distance. He kneeled by the side of the road, picking herbs. Alphonse was standing next to him. He must've gone to help after he got tired of waiting for Edward to finish with his checkup.

Edward started walking toward the two, breathing a light sigh. He and Alphonse weren't that different in age from the kids who'd been playing on the riverbank. If they hadn't left on this journey, they would be running home to eat donuts too when the skies looked like rain. Their quest had driven them so far from home, to this unknown land.

Edward was determined—they both were—but their journey had been harder than he could have imagined.

The first night out of Resembool, they had tried to stay in a hotel in a large town and been told that "no children without guardians are permitted to stay." Alphonse's appearance frightened both children and adults alike. No one believed him when he told them Alphonse was his brother, and the two were called liars almost daily. Once, when he tried to show his silver watch to preempt the usual comments, someone tried to rob them.

Everywhere they went, they were held back by what they were: children. Children traveling alone aren't allowed to stay in hotels. Children have no reason to travel alone, so they must be lying. Even if he is a state alchemist, he's a child. He's weak—an easy target.

Unlike back in Resembool, protected by the adults around them, Edward had learned for himself the hard way how cruel the world could be to a twelve-year-old.

Still he kept walking forward, in part out of an obligation to protect his brother. He had to. His brother looked bizarre and was the constant target of suspicion or, at best, inquisitive glances. He had chosen to join Edward on his journey even though he was still only eleven years old.

One other thing kept Edward's feet moving forward: he knew he couldn't go back.

Edward gripped his own shoulder with his Auto-Mail hand. He knew why Dr. Norm had tapped him on the shoulder. *Loosen up,* he was trying to say.

If only I could.

They were searching for something that might not even be real, and the road ahead of them was dark, yet he had to keep moving. They had no place to go home to. That's why he had burned the house where they grew up: So they wouldn't have a reason to look back over their shoulders. So they couldn't give up.

His silver watch marked the passage of time on this self-imposed exile. It wouldn't stop for injuries or colds. Edward took his hand off the shoulder and looked at the cold steel of his palm. "How can *this* loosen up?"

It was hard, knowing what he wanted, yet knowing it was still so far away. His hand and leg were still Auto-Mail, and his brother was still a walking suit of armor.

And here was his friend, a comrade in arms from Resembool, in this faraway land, walking steadily toward his own future. Gone were the gang of friends, playing, running in circles. Now they walked in a straight line, toward a clear goal.

"It's been a year already, and we're not any closer . . ."

Knowing what Pitt had been up to, seeing him act all adult-like, Edward felt himself being left behind. It bothered him more than he cared to admit.

Edward scowled up at the clouds hanging low over his head, then gritted his teeth and looked down at the road ahead.

A SHORT WHILE before Edward left the clinic, when the blue sky still peeked through the clouds, Alphonse played with some local kids on the riverbank. He looked up when he heard someone calling his name.

"Hey, Alphonse."

Pitt stood on top of the bridge, carrying a large basket in his hand.

"Hey there, Pitt."

Pitt looked down at Alphonse, half buried in the long reeds growing beside the river. The other kids hunkered beneath the bridge, their insect cages and nets in hand, parting the grass as they searched for their quarry.

"What'cha up to?"

"Waiting for Edward. Thought I'd help catch a few bugs to pass the time." Alphonse stood on his tiptoes and held up a small cage with a bright green grasshopper inside. It was particularly large. "Check it out. I caught it myself."

Next to him, the kids showed off their cages.

"Yours is the biggest after all, Alphonse. Mine's tiny," one boy said.

"Well, you told me where the best place to look was."

"Yeah, but it's hard to catch the big ones. They're clever."

The other kids nodded in agreement.

"Really?" Alphonse said, pointing to one of the boy's cages. "I think that butterfly you caught is prettier."

They all lifted their cages, comparing their catches and laughing.

They seemed like old friends, but it hadn't been this way from the start. Just a little while before, Alphonse had been standing on top of the bridge, waiting for his brother while the children played below, neither saying a word to the other.

Alphonse knew what they thought: other kids took one look at him and assumed he was an adult, and a stranger in town to boot. It was always difficult for him. He wanted to talk to kids his own age but found it impossible to start conversations if the kids were scared of him. He had tried various tactics in the past, but when he tried too hard to be friendly and calm their fears, it only made him seem more adult and defeated the purpose.

Still, though he looked a bit menacing on the outside, inside Alphonse remained only an eleven-year-old boy. As much as he tried to watch himself, he couldn't help chiming in when one of the boys on the riverbank caught a giant grasshopper.

"Cool!"

It turned out that was all it took to break the ice. One of the kids had invited him to come down, lending him a bug net and a cage. And so, Alphonse found himself playing with children his own age for the first time in recent memory while he waited for his brother.

"He'll be in there a little while longer," Pitt called down from the bridge. "Dr. Norm wasn't satisfied just checking out that cold—he's giving him the full rundown."

"Really? Good!" Alphonse said happily. Edward never went to the hospital when he could avoid it, even when he was hurt badly. As soon as he recovered from one altercation, he just went and got hurt again. Any opportunity for his brother to get a checkup was a good thing in Alphonse's eyes.

"Where are you off to, Pitt?"

"Doc wants me to fetch some medicinal herbs. They grow all over the village, so I just kind of make my rounds and pick what I can find."

"Can I help?" Alphonse offered. As long as they didn't stray too far, Edward would find him when he came out of the clinic.

"What about your bug hunt?"

"Oh, it's fine. Besides, I owe you for making that house call for us." Alphonse turned to the other kids. "I gotta go, guys."

"What? Leaving already?"

"Yeah, sorry. Let's hang out again, okay?" Alphonse apologized, and then began to look around. "I got this cage and net from Cassie . . . have you seen her?"

One of the boys pointed off toward town. "Cassie left for home already. It's her birthday tomorrow, and they're going on a shopping trip to the next town over. She's probably getting ready for the trip. I'll take her stuff, if you want."

"Thanks. Hey, give this grasshopper to her, would you?" Alphonse handed the boy his cage and net and walked up to the road to join Pitt. "Bye now!"

"See ya!"

"Yep, later!"

Alphonse waved back at them as he and Pitt marched back toward town. "Say, Pitt, do you know a girl named Cassie? I've never seen a girl who likes insects as much as her."

"Yeah . . ." Pitt stooped to examine some herbs growing by the side of the road.

"And I thought Winry was the only girl who wasn't afraid of bugs," Alphonse said with a laugh. "Remember when you and Edward threw all those pill bugs? And Winry . . ."

"Of all the things to remember." Pitt growled, casting a stare at Alphonse while his hands busily yanked some grasses up from the ground.

School had just started back up after vacation. One afternoon, Edward and Pitt skipped sweeping duty, and all the girls in class were yelling at them to clean up the room. In retrospect, the two boys were clearly in the wrong, but, at the time, it seemed more important that they fulfill their sacred role as school troublemakers. Their sworn mission was to get the girls riled up about *something*. Things had been too quiet, so they "forgot" to sweep. The girls yelled at them, so they plotted their revenge. This time, it involved them gathering up two heaping handfuls of pill bugs and, heedless of Alphonse's cries to stop, throwing them into the classroom.

The plan was a brilliant success. The girls who didn't scream outright skipped straight to crying. "Don't be such crybabies!" they shouted, clapping each other on the back.

Winry stood up to their attack, though—and launched a counterstrike of her own. After going around picking up all the pill bugs off the schoolroom floor, she snuck up behind the two as they stood atop the highest hill in town, basking in victory's warm glow, and crammed every last bug down their shirts.

Now, Edward and Pitt liked bugs, but there were limits. The two spent the better part of fifteen minutes running down the street, howling and squirming to reach the wriggling pill bugs in their shirts, pants, and shoes.

"I'll never forget the sound of you two screaming. I don't think anyone in town will . . ."

"That was a long time ago," Pitt scowled, shaking his head. He thrust his finger toward some yellow flowers growing in an open plot of land. "Hey, look. If you're really along to help out, why don't you pick those herbs . . . the ones way over there?"

Alphonse went to pick up the herbs, still talking. He didn't often have the chance to reminisce about home with someone other than his brother. "You and Ed fought a lot, but when it came to scheming up some wild plan, you were always in lockstep: our leaders to the end."

They may have been mean to the girls at school, but the antagonism was mutual. When it came to the younger kids, Edward and Pitt served as protectors, upholding schoolyard justice and fending off bullies. They were leaders, making up new games for everyone to play, though by the time everyone else starting playing them, they had already thought of something new to do. Alphonse remembered being envious of them. They always stayed one step ahead of everyone else.

"You ever play with those kids by the river? When you're not working, I mean."

Pitt shook his head. "I'm not a kid anymore, Alphonse. I don't have time to play."

"Really . . . I guess you must be pretty busy, what with the clinic and your studies and all," Alphonse said with a smile in his voice. Inside, he felt strangely lonely. Pitt wasn't much older than he was—only fourteen. He expected Pitt to be up to his old antics with the kids here, just like it had been in Resembool. Still, he couldn't help but be impressed at how much progress Pitt had made toward a career.

Alphonse threw some herbs into Pitt's basket and pointed at his friend's glasses. "I bet your eyes went bad from studying too hard. It's funny—they make you look different—more grown up."

"Well, you haven't changed a bit," Pitt said with a wry smile, looking up at Alphonse. He pushed his glasses back up onto his nose. "You always were good at making friends."

Indeed, back in Resembool, Alphonse had always been the one to break the ice whenever a new kid came to town. Things had been different on the road, however. He shook his head. "Not too long ago, I might've told you you were wrong."

"What do you mean?"

Alphonse nodded. "Look at me. When we're out on the road, people would say all kinds of things to me. They'd

tell me how scary-looking I was. No one believes I'm only eleven—especially not kids my own age. I can't change how I look, of course, so I always tried to change how I acted. But back by the river, I realized I was doing things the wrong way. When I talked to those kids just now, everything was fine. They let me play with them, and we had a good time. I just spoke to them like a normal kid.

"It made me realize that when things went bad in the past, it was partly my fault. I started to expect people to be scared, and I would say something a little odd or act a little nervous . . . and of course that just leads to an odd, nervous sort of conversation. I guess the trick is not to worry so much," Alphonse said, feeling a weight lift off his shoulders. Playing with kids his own age after such a long time finally made him realize what a burden loneliness could be. "I'm sure it's been the same with you, Pitt, but leaving Resembool and meeting all these strangers . . . I've learned a lot. But it hasn't all been fun, either."

"Yeah, I know," Pitt said, quietly. He knew all too well what it was like to leave your home and try to make it in the wide world. Suddenly, he turned and slapped Alphonse on the back. "You know, I'm impressed. I never thought of you as anything other than Edward's little brother, but you've really grown."

"Heh, thanks," Alphonse said with a chuckle. The way Pitt slapped his back reminded him of Edward. "You know,

I really owe it all to Ed, though. Whenever I lose my way, he's there to pat me on the back and point me in the right direction. It keeps me going. I know it's been hard for him too, but he hasn't complained once since he left Resembool. Not a single time . . . "

Alphonse looked off into the distance at an abandoned house on the far side of the field in which they stood. "He's so much more together than when we were in Resembool, it almost makes me worry more. Of course, he's still a little headstrong and reckless, that hasn't changed."

Pitt had been walking along looking for herbs, his face toward the ground, but now he looked up. "You haven't been back to Resembool?"

"No."

"Not even once?"

Alphonse chuckled. "Nope. I'm always trying to get him to go back sometime to see how Pinako and Winry are doing, but Ed shakes his head and says we should keep going until we've done what we set out to do. Still, it'd be nice if we could drop by someday when we're in the area. How about you, Pitt? You go back sometimes?"

"Well, no," Pitt mumbled, frowning slightly.

"What's wrong?" Alphonse cast a curious look downward and caught Pitt glaring back up at him.

"Don't peer down at me like that."

"Oh, sorry."

"You always were taller than me. It's annoying." Pitt looked away, pouting his lips.

"Not again! You and Ed worry about that way too much, really."

"Easy for you to say. You're tall! For us, it's a serious problem, no . . ." Pitt chuckled. "Well, maybe it's more of a serious problem for Edward than it is for me."

"Come on, you're not *that* far apart, if at all . . ." Alphonse began when Pitt reached up and grabbed his neck and began shaking him.

"Hah! It's clear that I am the taller one! Anyone can see that!"

"Well, we've never been able to measure it properly . . ."

"Okay, you want proper? How about I mark my height on your armor now, and then we'll trick Edward into marking his. Compare the marks, and presto! Not even Edward will be able to deny the truth then!"

"Hey, no scribbling on my armor, please."

"It's not scribbling. This is a serious scientific inquiry! Look, I promise I'll wipe it off later. Come on, please! I want to prove, once and for all, that Edward's the runt, not me." Pitt grinned and, beneath the rapidly darkening cloudy sky, he produced a ruler and pen from his shirt pocket.

"I don't think that's such a good idea . . ." Alphonse said, trying to dodge to one side, when they heard footsteps approaching from the distance. From the sound of it, whoever the footsteps belonged to was coming *fast*.

"Who're you calling a runt?!"

"Ack, Edward!"

"Hey, Ed!"

Alphonse and Pitt looked up to see the Fullmetal Alchemist bearing down at them, his face a livid shade of red. "I heard you!"

Like Alphonse, Edward had been doing some thinking of his own about their year on the road. Wanting a little more time alone, he didn't run up to his brother and Pitt when he spotted them in the distance. Instead, he took his time, walking along behind them slowly. He was getting closer and was just about to call out to them when a chance wind carried a single word down the road to his ears: "runt."

Ed broke into a full-out charge, straight toward Pitt. "Hrrah!" He ran without slowing until the last minute, when he kicked at the ground and flew through the air at his target, his knee bent before him. It was an attack with which Pitt was intimately familiar. He was ready.

"Flying kick this!" he shouted, tossing his basket of herbs to one side and crossing his arms in front of him to block Edward's foot. "Same pattern of attack, every time!" He caught Edward's knee expertly in his hands and chuckled. They had fought so many times in the past, they knew each other's style down to the last move.

But Edward, still in midair, his knee caught between Pitt's hands, had a victorious grin on his face. "Oh, yeah? Well, you always use the same pattern of defense!" Edward's hand arched out and came down on Pitt's forehead. "Take that!"

There was a satisfying *slap.*

"Ouch!" Pitt wailed, rubbing his forehead. Edward dropped lightly to the ground. His slap had been hard enough to leave a red blotch and make Pitt's eyes water. "Grr . . . Nice! A two-part attack!"

"You like?" Edward laughed instantly, forgetting his brooding concern about his lack of progress over the year. "Okay, runt of Resembool! Let's have a confession, right here, right now. Al can be the witness!"

"Um, I didn't sign up for this." Alphonse sighed, warily eyeing his brother, standing victoriously before Pitt, who still cradled his head in his hands. He took a step back. In any other situation, now would be the time for Alphonse to intervene, but he knew instinctively that once the word *runt* was in play, his best move was to disengage and let them at it. As if to confirm this, Pitt pulled his hand off his forehead and immediately balled it into a fist, and the battle was rejoined.

"You're the runt, Edward!"

"Dream on, Pitt!"

"Just admit it, already, Ed-runt!"

"You admit it, Pitt-shrimp!"

So they shouted back and forth, each one looking for an opening in the other's defenses. When Pitt swung a punch, Edward blocked it. When Edward tried to sweep Pitt's feet out from underneath him, Pitt deftly stomped on his toes.

Still, even though they knew each other's moves, it was not an even match. Though it had only been a year, Edward's time in the military had paid off. He was the stronger and better fighter of the two, and Pitt sensed it. Pitt drew back, putting distance between them, and took up a defensive stance. "You been training?" He called out, "Well, so have I. Here, I'll show you!" Stooping down, Pitt tore a small bush of berries up from the grass at his feet, and threw it toward Edward.

"Oh, now you're throwing weeds?" Edward sneered, dodging to the side. Some of the berries broke off the bush and scattered across his legs.

"Huh?" As the berries hit him, they began to swell. "Ow, ow, ow!" The next instant, the berries exploded with a sound like firecrackers, splattering their hard thorny skins over his legs and arms.

"See that? All it takes is a little jolt, and they pop . . . and you can brew them to make a great tea for a sore throat! It's a new strain, just developed! Take that!" Pitt snatched up another handful of the berries and threw them at his now-cowering opponent.

The berries hurt more than he could believe. Edward ducked and dodged, yelling, "That stings! If you're going to use your herbs on me, I'll use my alchemy!"

"What?!" A look of panic came into Pitt's eyes. Since Resembool, even the threat of alchemy had usually been enough to bring a fight to an abrupt end. Possessing an alchemical power strong enough to earn a teenager the title of state alchemist made it clear even to an amateur's eyes that he was out of his league.

"Hey, no fair!" Pitt protested, "I thought alchemy was to help the masses! Well, I'm one of the masses!"

"Hah, nice try!"

"Yipes! No, wait . . ."

Standing a short distance from the furious battle, Alphonse sighed. Edward and Pitt, patient and doctor, had completely forgotten everything but their fight. "I guess I should just let them get it out of their systems," Alphonse muttered, picking up the basket that Pitt had thrown aside. He resumed walking, looking for the herbs Pitt had taught him to find.

When he next looked up, he found he was standing near the entrance to the old coal mine. His eyes fell on a large boulder about ten feet high, sitting directly in front of the entrance to the path that led down into the mineshaft. A rail emerged from the middle of the boulder going toward the mine. *That rail must be for a mining cart of some sort.*

But now, most of the rail had been ripped up. Rust caked on what few parts remained. Large boards had been placed in an "X" over the entrance to the mine, and the inside was too dim to clearly see. Where miners' feet once tread, now thick green grass grew, covering everything. Several different kinds of flowers swayed gently in the breeze.

Thinking that some of them might be the medicinal herbs he was looking for, Alphonse stepped toward the mine. He began to move the flowers aside with his hand when he heard a pleasant voice in front of him.

"Oh! Alphonse!"

Alphonse looked up to see a young girl emerge from the old mine entrance—the same young girl he had been catching bugs with beneath the bridge.

"Cassie!"

She worked her way out from between the boards. She looked every part the quintessential tomboy, with wavy blond hair cut short and a boy's shirt and trousers.

" . . . Cassie?!"

Pitt, who still wrestled with Edward a short distance away, saw Cassie, and his expression changed in an instant.

She looked past Alphonse and spotted him. "Pitt!"

Seeing Cassie break into a run, Pitt hastily extricated himself from Edward's grasp. "Sorry, gotta take a rain check on this one! If she catches me, I'll never get rid of her." He bolted down the hill.

"Huh? Hey!" Edward called after him, "If you chicken out now, that's as good as admitting you're the runt!"

"Fat chance! I'll prove it beyond a doubt—next time, you just wait!"

Edward, furious, stood waving his fist in the air at the rapidly receding Pitt. "What's with him . . . Hey!" Something impacted with Edward's back, just above his waist. He looked around.

"Hey, where's Pitt?! Where'd he go?" Cassie asked, pulling on Edward's shirt. She looked around, but Pitt was already out of sight.

"Uh, Pitt left. Did you need something from him?"

"Yes! He has to make me medicine!"

"Medicine?"

Alphonse walked up beside Edward. "Hey, Cassie. Thanks for letting me borrow your net and stuff back at the bridge." Alphonse looked back at the boards covering the mine entrance. "What are you doing out here? I thought you had to get ready for some trip tomorrow?"

"I don't know if I'll be able to go," she said.

"Huh?"

"Danny had another one of his coughing fits. Mom took him to Dr. Norm's right away, but she gets all worried. Anyway, it doesn't matter. I did kinda want a birthday present, though . . ."

"Danny? I think I just saw him down at the clinic. Is he your brother?"

Cassie nodded.

"The clinic? What, is he sick?"

Edward shook his head. "The doctor said it's a condition he was born with. He gave him some medicine though. If that stops his coughing, won't you be able to go tomorrow?"

Cassie shook her head. "No, no way. When Danny gets bad, Dad and Mom barely go out for a week. We had to cancel a picnic just the other month. I tell them we can still go out if we bring the medicine with us, but they don't think so."

"Hmm," Edward thought, recalling his conversation with Dr. Norm. "Yeah, he did say that Danny's medicine was pretty strong stuff." So strong that Pitt wasn't allowed to hand it out, and Dr. Norm avoided using it when he could. It was probably expensive too—not the kind of medicine you just threw in a bag for a day trip. Suddenly, it occurred to Edward why Cassie was looking for Pitt. "So you want Pitt to make you something with his herbs?"

"Yeah. I've heard him talking about herbal remedies before, how they're good for curing all sorts of things, even coughs like Danny's. If we had some herbs to use, that'd be way cheaper than the medicine from the clinic, and we could maybe even use them on a trip . . ."

If he wasn't seriously ill, then a natural, more gentle cure did sound better than the processed medicine his mother always gave him. But one thing troubled Edward: if there were a medicinal herb that could help Danny, why wouldn't Pitt prepare it for her?

"Lately, he runs away as soon as he sees me. It's not nice," Cassie said, looking angry.

"That's funny." Edward scratched his head. "I thought Pitt's whole reason for being here was to make herbal medicine." Hadn't the doctor said that Pitt saw the value in cheaper alternatives to pharmaceuticals, with gentler effects? Wasn't he learning about herbs for the very purpose of helping the weak and the poor? There must be some reason he would refuse to make medicine for Danny, other than simply not wanting to.

"I'm sure he's not being mean on purpose," Alphonse said, consoling the girl. "Maybe they're just aren't any of those good herbs for coughs around here." He glanced again toward the mine entrance. "Anyway, Cassie . . . isn't it dangerous here? I mean, is it really safe to go in that mine?" Though the entrance to the mine had maintained its shape, sections were beginning to crumble.

Edward agreed. "If there were a cave-in, you'd be in a lot of danger. Don't they tell the people in town to stay away?" That was surely the reason for the boards.

Cassie blushed. "Well, yeah, but . . ." she began, pouting her lips. "But this is my secret hideout."

"Hideout?"

She sighed. "It's just no fun being at home all the time. Just today, I tried to show Mom the grasshopper I caught, but she was too busy taking care of Danny to pay any attention to me. When I catch a big stag beetle, or get some pretty beads, or find a weird shaped rock, it's always the same. Dad and Mom never look at my things. That's why I hide all my best stuff here. No one's going to look at it anyway. And . . ." Suddenly the strength went out of Cassie's voice and she began to tremble. "And Mom and Dad only love Danny anyway. That's why I made a secret place just for me. This is my real house! I want to live here forever!" Cassie choked back a sob.

Cassie knew they had to take care of her weak younger brother. That's why she hounded Pitt to make her medicine for Dan. But the broken promise to go buy a birthday present, combined with Pitt running away again, was too much to take. Talking to Edward and Alphonse brought everything she had been holding inside to the surface.

The brothers exchanged glances.

They were thinking the same thing. Cassie seemed like such a lively girl, happy to run around catching insects with the boys, and yet she came all the way up here to hide. How unwanted she must feel to make this abandoned mine her home.

"Cassie . . ." Alphonse gently rubbed Cassie's head. Her shoulders heaved with each sobbing breath.

Alphonse knew he had to say something. Whenever it came to consoling someone, Edward was terrible. He would either push them away or go on the offensive.

But it was Edward who spoke first.

"Don't cry." His voice was quiet. "I'm sure your Mom and Dad love you very much. Your family. You should go home. Look, we'll even walk you there." Edward said, reaching out to take the little girl's hand.

But Cassie angrily brushed him away. "No, I don't want to go home. I'm going to live here!" With each of Cassie's sobs, a tear rolled down her cheek and fell on the ground, making a little wet spot. Soon the circle of spots widened until they were surrounded by them.

"Hey, it's raining," Alphonse looked up at the sky. The swollen clouds hung low, and large droplets of rain had begun to fall.

"Right," said Edward, "you better get home, Cassie. What would happen if Danny got all better tomorrow, and you couldn't go because you caught a cold in the rain!"

"It doesn't matter," she said. "Dad and Mom wouldn't even notice if I didn't come home. They're only worried about Danny."

Edward looked down at her, then he dropped to one knee to bring his eyes level with hers. "Cassie, when you come home after playing outside, is the door locked? Is there no dinner waiting for you?" He put his hand on her little head and stared into teary eyes. "No, there's food, and the door is open. That's because your Dad and Mom are waiting for you. That's where you belong, okay?"

Large tears streamed from Cassie's big eyes, she looked down at the ground, but Edward could sense a reaction in her to his words.

Cassie looked back. "You don't think they forgot about me? They don't hate me?"

"Of course they don't. Even when Danny's not doing well, and they're worried about him, they wouldn't forget you."

"Really?"

"Really. How about this: you go home, and when you go inside, say 'Hi, I'm home!' real loud. I bet they'll say hi back. If they didn't like you or they'd forgotten you, they wouldn't say anything."

Edward grabbed Cassie's hand again. This time she didn't push him away.

By the time they reached the Rhymar household at the edge of town, the rain came down in hard, punishing sheets. Under the sheet of gray clouds, everything seemed dark and lifeless, save for the light streaming from the windows of the house.

Cassie let go of Edward and Alphonse's hands, and looked up at them. "Thanks," she said. Her eyes were dry.

"Later," Edward said, giving her another pat on the head. Cassie smiled faintly and ran toward her house.

Edward knew it must take a lot of effort to overcome feeling lonely in your own home, but if anybody had the energy to do it, Cassie did.

As they watched, she bounded up the front steps, opened the front door, and went inside.

"Hi, I'm home!"

ONCE THE RAIN started falling, it didn't stop. It grew harder and harder throughout the afternoon and well into the night.

Alphonse sat outside the door to their borrowed house, watching the rain splash into puddles for a while. "It's really coming down out there," he announced as he stepped back into the room. "If it's raining like this tomorrow, we won't be able to leave no matter how good you feel."

"Says you. I don't care if there's a flood out there, we're leaving," Edward declared from the bed. "That medicine Dr. Norm gave me worked like a charm. I'm not staying in this town any longer."

Even after the drenching on the way back from Cassie's house, Edward's cold seemed none the worse for wear. He did seem to be getting better. "I think we should head farther west next. There was a big town out that way, wasn't there? Might get a lead on the Philosopher's Stone," he said, eager to get back on the road. Seeing how far Pitt had come in the year made him want to make some progress of his own as soon as possible.

But this was one of those rare occasions where Alphonse had a different idea. "How about we go back to Resembool first?"

"Resembool?" Edward asked, still facing the wall, his back turned to his brother.

"Yeah. We should go home every once in a while. You need a maintenance check on your Auto-Mail anyway."

"Why would I want that? It's not broken. And there are plenty of other places I'd rather go. We don't have time to go home."

"If you say so . . . " Alphonse realized that talking about the old days with Pitt had made him homesick. He shook this feeling off and tried changing the subject. "I was surprised you were so nice to Cassie. We might never have gotten her home if you hadn't stepped in."

"Hey, I'm always nice."

"Right, funny. Remember when Winry used to fall down and cry? You'd call her a crybaby . . . and make her cry even harder."

"Ancient history," Edward snorted, glaring at his brother over his shoulder. The particular incident Alphonse recalled had happened before they were even in school. And Edward

hadn't intended to make her cry more. He just didn't understand how to make her stop. "I was just trying to help her out."

"Kind of an interesting way to help."

Edward frowned. "Look, I'm going to bed," he said, pulling
the covers over his head.

"I've just been thinking about the past a lot since running
into Pitt," Alphonse went on. "Remember that time when you
wet the bed? You hung your sheets outside in the rain, and
Winry saw them. You got so flustered that you just started
babbling, and . . ."

"If you have to remember something, remember anything
but that!"

"Whoa!" Alphonse shouted as Edward's wadded-up blanket came careening toward his head. "Hey, if you're planning
on resting up, don't go throwing away your blankets," he
admonished, gently returning the blankets to his brother's
bed. Edward thrust his head under his pillow.

"Get some sleep. I'm going to go see Pitt."

"Pitt?" Edward looked up to see Alphonse picking up a
basket by the door. It was the one Pitt had been using to
gather his medicinal herbs.

"When he ran away from Cassie, he forgot to take his basket.
The herbs got a little wet in the rain, but I think they've dried
off well enough now. I'm going to take them to him."

"Want me to come along?"

Edward did feel at least partly responsible that the herbs

got wet. If Alphonse hadn't joined Edward to walk Cassie back home, he might have reached their house before the rain started falling in earnest. Edward sat up in bed, but Alphonse waved his hand and walked toward the door. "No, I couldn't force a sick man out in weather like this . . . even if you do really, *really* like the rain."

"But . . ." Edward began, still concerned, and then his brother's choice of words hit him. "Grr . . . Al!" Edward shot out of bed, but the door had already shut. His shouting echoed around the house, chasing after Alphonse as he left.

"SOMETIMES, I wish he didn't have such a good memory . . ."

Alone in the house, Edward grumbled to himself, tossing and turning beneath his blanket. Not that he could blame his brother—that day remained burned vividly into his own mind, too.

It had been drizzling the entire morning after Edward wet the bed, but he hung his sheets outside anyway in an attempt to hide the evidence. It would have worked, too, if Winry hadn't happened by just as he and Alphonse were heading out for a walk.

"Why are your sheets hanging outside? They're going to get wet."

"Oh, yeah, I know."

"Aren't you gonna take them in?"

"No . . . I, uh, like the rain."

"Enough to sleep in it?"
"Yeah. I really, really like the rain."

Edward looked up at the ceiling. "Winry . . ."

Something inside Edward had clicked when Alphonse mentioned going back to Resembool. They had talked about it many times before, but every time he let it blow by. If there were a problem with his Auto-Mail or Alphonse really wanted to go home, he might have given it serious consideration, but as it was, it didn't make sense going so far out of their way for anything less than an emergency.

"I wonder if she still cries so much."

Edward remembered the day he called Winry a crybaby. Eventually, it *had* gotten her to stop. She had been so mad, she stood up and smacked Edward in the jaw.

It wasn't like that the day they left the village, when Winry stood crying in front of their burning house. Not sure what to do, he had once again said the first thing that came to mind. "You always were a crybaby." It didn't make her stop then, and he couldn't make her more angry than she already was. Edward never told her why they were leaving, and Winry had waved good-bye to them without asking the hundreds of questions he could see in her eyes.

"What if she cries again? And where would we stay? It's been a whole year, and nothing's changed. We can't go back to Resembool."

Edward closed his eyes, listening to the sound of the rain beating down on the roof.

"ED! ED, wake up!"

"Huh? What? Oh, it's you, Al . . ." Edward groggily rubbed his eyes, and rolled over in bed. "It morning already? Let's get ready to leave . . ."

"No, it's not morning—just get up!" Alphonse shouted, shaking his brother roughly by the shoulder.

Edward opened his eyes, realizing for the first time that something was wrong. Alphonse never shook him like that. "What is it, Al?"

Edward felt like he had been asleep for long time. He half-expected to find the morning light streaming through the window, yet the room seemed as dark now as it had been when he fell asleep. The sound of the rain on the roof was even louder than before.

"Ed, come on! The river . . ."

"River?" Edward put one and one together. "What? Is it flooding?!"

"Not yet, but it's only a matter of time!"

Edward ran to the door, peering out into the rainy gloom. He immediately noticed that the river seemed much closer than it had that morning. The water level must have risen considerably. The gentle flow from before was gone, replaced with a wild torrent crested with the white edges of swirling waves. By the sides of the river, several lanterns hanging from poles swung wildly in the wind.

"The townsfolk have started piling up sandbags along the riverbanks, but I don't know how long that will hold!"

When Alphonse went to bring the basket to the clinic, he had found Dr. Norm working with the other villagers in the steadily increasing downpour to raise the banks of the river. He was dripping from head to toe. "The reservoir upstream has burst its dam!"

The dirt walls of the reservoir typically held strong against slight increases in the water level and even the light floods of spring. If the reservoir dam had broken, no matter how high they raised the banks of the river, it wouldn't be high enough. Alphonse ran to get his brother.

"I can't do it myself! You have to help, Ed!"

"Right!" Edward shouted, finally understanding what his brother wanted. Whipping on his coat, he dashed out into the rain. "Looks like the time to pay back the town's hospitality came sooner than we thought!"

The two made their way down the road, which was a sodden mess, and soon their feet were caked in mud. The ground, already so saturated that it was almost like a river of mud itself, was far too wet to draw an alchemical circle on. Only Edward, who could do alchemy without the aid of the circle, had any hope of raising a dike to keep the water in the river from spilling out.

As they slogged their way through the mud toward the river, they could hear the adults from town shouting.

"Arrgh! No good! The water keeps rising!"

"Raise the banks as high as you can!"

"Can't let the fields get drenched this close to harvest time!"

Every able-bodied man in town heaved massive sandbags, piling them by the edge of the river, but already the water threatened to overflow their hastily constructed wall.

Edward and Alphonse ran between larger men carrying heavy bags of dirt on their shoulders and made for the bridge.

"Uh-oh, that looks bad!" As the brothers watched, the level of the water rose until it almost reached the bridge. "It's gotten higher since I went to get you!"

The river here had become a roaring torrent. The high reeds on the bank where Alphonse had been catching bugs were already swamped with water, and the water was sloshing up against the base of the bridge.

"It may already be too high to stop it with dikes," Edward shouted. Next to him, Pitt arrived with several children in tow.

"Edward! Alphonse!"

"Pitt! Is the clinic all right?"

"No idea! I was afraid the water was going to come in, so I brought the kids out here!"

The ground level on the far side of the bridge seemed to be lower than the near side, and Edward could see the water already spilling out in sheets toward the town.

Pitt, rain dripping from his glasses, told the kids with him to head up the hill, then ran back to the bridge. On top, Dr. Norm helped guide women and children out of the village. Next to him stood a huddle of children too terrified of the river's wrath to move. The reservoir had never broken before, and they had never seen such a flood.

"I'll be right there!" Alphonse shouted, running for the bridge. Edward joined him, and together with Pitt and Dr. Norm, they began pushing the children across to safety.

"There you go! Just a little farther!"

"We'll all be safe on the hill!"

Those they couldn't convince to walk, Alphonse picked up. "Let's get out of here!"

"Pitt, Edward, get off the bridge. It's too dangerous!" Dr. Norm shouted. The sound of rushing water suddenly increased. The torrent below surged up and struck the underside of the bridge. Great volumes of water blasted onto the other side, streaming through the fields toward . . .

"The clinic!" One of the men packing sandbags by the river shouted in alarm. "Wait, Danny's medicine! Doctor, what about Danny's medicine?!" The man who must have been Danny's father threw down his shovel.

Dr. Norm looked back from where he'd been helping a handful of stragglers toward the hill. It looked clear that no one had time to worry about medicine. "Let it go!" Dr. Norm shouted, shaking his head furiously in the rain. "We can get more medicine soon, and the herbs we have will work for Danny's cough!"

"But . . ." Danny's father frowned and turned back toward the bridge. His face looked stricken with unease at the thought of losing the one curative that could stop Danny's coughing fits immediately. "Doctor, what kind of bottle is the medicine in?!"

By now, the water had risen so high that going back to the clinic looked like a one-way trip.

"You can't go back—the bridge could fall any minute!" Dr. Norm shouted, but the man still seemed unconvinced.

"I'll go get it!" shouted a voice in front of Edward, who was busily trying to figure out a way to raise a dike in the mud. It was Pitt. "I know where Danny's medicine is! I'll be right back!"

But as Pitt tried to cross the bridge, Danny's father grabbed his arm. "No!" A hard look on his face, the man dragged Pitt back down from the bridge. "You can't do this! You need to get to safety with the other children!"

His tone made it clear that he wasn't stopping Pitt out of concern for Pitt's safety. He was stopping Pitt because he didn't believe the boy could do any good.

Even Edward could see Pitt's face twist behind his dripping glasses. Edward was frowning, too. He expected Pitt to lash back, but much to his surprise, his friend quietly replaced his glasses and hurried back to the safe side of the bridge, with Danny's father behind him. Again, the water slammed against the bottom of the bridge. A surge just above the bridge knocked the sandbags off the wall, and water went streaming out into a field.

"The sandbags aren't holding!"

"Everyone back!"

The remaining men dropped their sandbags and retreated from the river's edge. The water slowly seeped into the village. They watched in pain as the ripe wheat and vegetables in their fields were lost beneath the muddy swirls.

But while the townspeople headed up to the hill, Edward alone went back down to the river.

This bridge is coming down soon!

If the support posts of the bridge gave out, it would make a hole in the wall of sandbags, and the river would flow straight out into town.

Edward looked back over his shoulder at Alphonse helping the children up the path away from the river. If the wall broke, then the flat fields and roads of the town would be submerged immediately, and anyone not on the hill would be washed away.

"I can't use this wet mud to make a dike—it will just wash away too quickly. So what do I . . . " Edward's brain churned as he looked around. He saw an open field a little way down the river. An idea came to him. *Don't know if I can do this, but it's worth a shot!*

Running down to where the river curved slightly before the field, Edward stepped forward and brought his hands together with a loud clap.

The townspeople still near the river shouted at him.

"What is he doing?!"

"Hey you, the river is about to flood over!"

"Get away from there!"

Without looking back, Edward thrust his hands into the rushing river. "Everyone, get back!" he shouted at them, as a great light flared from his hands.

In the blaze of light, a section of the river bank at the corner began to sink. Soon the entire empty field became a great hollow in the muddy ground, into which the water from the river rushed.

Drawn off by the sudden appearance of a new pond, the surge of water beneath the bridge lessened.

"Great, it worked! Okay . . ."

Edward looked away from the submerged field, and this time, the alchemical light that had created the pond raced along the river's edge like a thunderbolt. Now all the earth that had moved out to make the pond thrust up in a great muddy wall.

"And . . . done!"

The light faded, and the sound of the beating rain and gloom once again settled on the town—and its newly constructed dike and reservoir. Though the rushing water had chewed away at the wet soil along the banks, the reservoir sapped enough of its strength to prevent the river from breaking through Edward's dike and the wall of sandbags.

"W-was that alchemy?!"

"Amazing!"

The villagers turned to Edward in astonishment.

"It's little more than a stopgap, but I think it should hold. We'd better reinforce it while we have a chance," he told them as Danny's father and the other men snapped out of their daze and began to speak all at once.

"Simply incredible! I had no idea you were an alchemist!"

"Here we thought you were just some sick boy passing through!"

"Look, the water's draining from the fields!"

"The clinic was spared the worst of it too! Hey, Rhymar, looks like Danny's medicine will be okay! Good for you!"

"I was just about ready to give up on the harvest this year! Thank you!"

As the villagers came streaming back from the hill they all shouted their thanks, smiles of joy on every face. Danny's father shook Edward's hand.

The breaking of the reservoir dam and the flood had been entirely unexpected. The villagers had reacted as best they could, but even as they began building the sandbag walls, they knew it was too little, too late. Yet, when a natural disaster seemed inevitable, a single young boy had come to the town's rescue. For an entire town wondering how they would make it through the next winter, it was a miracle.

Smiling and laughing, the men went back to work, carrying sandbags to reinforce the dike.

"Good job, Ed!" Alphonse called out. He was carrying the boy Danny on his back. "That was a good idea, making that reservoir."

"Al," Edward said, raising an eyebrow, "you sure you should be carrying Danny out in this rain?"

"He's got a raincoat on, so we're fine, but he got drenched on the way up to the hill. His mother wanted me to take him to see Dr. Norm. At least he's not coughing."

From Alphonse's back, Danny reached out a small hand toward Edward. "You saved my medicine! Thanks!" He had been watching Edward's alchemy from the hill, and though he was too young to understand what had happened, Alphonse had filled him in.

"Yeah, the medicine's fine," Edward said, giving Danny's hand a shake, but then the boy frowned.

"I don't like that medicine. It's yucky. I like Pitt's medicine better."

"Huh? You mean Pitt actually made medicine for you?" Alphonse asked, remembering what Cassie had said. He turned to look at Pitt, standing a short distance away. He stood alone, staring up at the dike Edward had made with his alchemy. In the midst of all the excitement and happiness, Pitt alone looked like he had swallowed something bitter.

"Hey, Pitt. What's wrong?" Edward asked walking over, thinking his friend must be down after what Danny's father had said to him.

Pitt slowly turned his gaze from the makeshift reservoir to stare at Edward. "She did this too, didn't she. The alchemist you apprenticed yourself to?"

"Huh? Oh, yeah, you're right. I guess she did."

Pitt was talking about Izumi, the woman who had come to Resembool once during a rainstorm. As Edward had done today, she too had constructed larger dikes with alchemy to hold back the river there. Impressed, Edward and Alphonse had asked to become her apprentices and studied under her for a while.

"Funny, I hadn't noticed that I was copying her until you mentioned it."

"You did more than that. You added the reservoir, too . . ."

"Yeah, but Izumi's dike was huge—much bigger than mine. I *am* still in training, after all."

Edward wasn't just being modest. Izumi's alchemy was of the highest order, and though he might mimic it, his attempts would never reach her level without years more training.

Pitt frowned and turned away. "Oh, yeah. Like you need to get better than that," he mumbled, raising his hand to fix his glasses.

Edward had trouble hearing what he said through the rain and the muffling effect of Pitt's hand.

"Huh? You say something?"

Suddenly Pitt whirled and slapped Edward on the cheek.

"Yowch!" Edward yelped, so surprised he sat down in the mud. When he looked up, he was furious. "What's the big idea?!"

"What's wrong, Pitt?!" Alphonse asked from behind them.

"How can you say that?" Pitt asked, his voice a growl. "Still in training? Well it was good enough to save that medicine—the medicine I couldn't save . . . !"

Edward could see Pitt was biting his lip and his hands were trembling—but he wasn't about to take this abuse quietly. He had been expecting at least a word of thanks for helping out, not *this*. "What's gotten into you? Who cares about protecting that crappy medicine? You can make your own!"

"What do you know about it?"

"Enough to know you're angry at me over something that's not my fault!" Edward jumped to his feet, ready to take a swing, when Alphonse ran between them, still carrying Danny on his back. "Stop fighting! C'mon, the flood's been averted, and the town's been saved. We should be celebrating along with everyone else!"

"Feh." Pitt spat and turned away. He looked down at the ground, ignoring Edward, who stood with fists raised, like a boxer before a big match.

"What, you running?" Edward taunted him, but Pitt didn't look around.

"I'm not running from anything. I'm going to check on the herbs around town, see if they're okay," Pitt replied in a low voice. Then he picked up his lamp and walked away.

"What's with him . . . ?" Edward muttered, slowly cooling down from his battle mode.

"Your cheek okay?" Alphonse asked, sliding Danny higher

up on his back. "I need to get this kid to the doctor, anyway. Why don't you come along too, Ed. And no fighting, 'kay?"

"Fine," Edward mumbled back. He'd been ready to chase after Pitt and beat him down to the ground right there, but Alphonse had seen right through him and cut him off. Edward half considered running down Pitt anyway, but in the end he decided that he'd already given his younger brother enough trouble since they had come to town.

"It was pretty strange of Pitt to just hit you like that, though," Alphonse said as they walked. "You should ask him why he did it. Later, though, when he's cooled off."

"You bet I'll ask him! I'll ask him five times, one for each knuckle!" Edward said, raising his clenched fist. The brothers walked toward the bridge. Across the river, they could see lights on at the clinic. Dr. Norm must be back at work already.

As they crossed the bridge, Edward and Alphonse lowered their lamps and looked down at the river below. The water was brown with mud, but it rushed by without threatening to touch the bridge or its new banks.

At the clinic, the herbs in the garden by the front door had been bent over by the water. When they opened the door, they found that some water had seeped in and pooled on the floor of the clinic. However, the damage to the garden seemed superficial, and the floor would be good as new after a thorough mopping.

"Dr. Norm?" Alphonse called out to the doctor, who was

busily sweeping water out a back door using a long board.

"Ah! Alphonse and Edward, I see."

"Do you think you could take a look at Danny? He got pretty wet before we found him a raincoat."

"Of course, of course. Let's see how your brother's cold is coming while we're at it, shall we?"

Dr. Norm led them into the examination room straight-away, and after sitting Danny in front of a small heater, he gave Edward's chest a listen with his stethoscope. "Pitt told me you were an alchemist, but to be honest, I never expected anything of that caliber. You've done this town a great service. Everyone thanks you."

"Good job, Ed," Alphonse said happily, knowing full well that his brother hadn't done it for the attention, but feeling no small amount of fraternal pride at the same time. "Danny's mother was watching from the hill—she was so happy. She said she'd be here later after going to pick up Cassie, and she wanted to thank you personally."

"I'll pass," Edward said glumly. "Wait, is Cassie home alone?"

"Yeah. She went home as soon as the dike went up. Her dad was still piling sandbags, and her mom planned on bringing Danny in, but I suggested that she go pick Cassie up first—we didn't know how long Danny's checkup would take, and I figured Cassie could play with us and Pitt while she waited."

Edward allowed himself a relieved breath. It surprised him,

how concerned he was about the little girl they had met earlier that day, and he was glad his brother had maneuvered to keep her from being stuck alone again in her own house.

Dr. Norm slapped a poultice on Edward's cheek. "You get into a fight or something?"

His cheek had swollen where Pitt slapped it, and it was beginning to throb painfully.

"It wasn't a fight. Pitt just decked me out of nowhere! He's got one coming to him as soon as I get out of here."

Dr. Norm took off his stethoscope and chuckled. "You got a little rained on, but it looks like you beat that cold, Edward. You can leave tomorrow if you like—just don't push yourself, okay?" Dr. Norm patted Edward gently on the shoulder.

"Thanks for everything," Edward said, remembering the doctor's advice from before. He had to learn how to take a breath every now and then, even on this seemingly endless journey. He was lucky that they had happened to run into a doctor who was good not only at examining cuts and bruises but weary hearts as well. On the mend, and with a clean bill of health, Edward felt good. He yawned.

Still, good health didn't necessarily mean he was happy. "Now I got to go find Pitt and deck him one!" No matter how eager he was to leave town, there was business to settle first—business between his fist and Pitt's jaw.

"What did I say now? No fights. You all play nice, understand? Isn't that right, Danny?" Dr. Norm said, listening to the boy's chest through his stethoscope.

Danny nodded. "Yeah. Cassie says that all the time. And if she can't go shopping tomorrow, we're gonna play."

"Really, now?"

"Good to hear," Alphonse said, looking at his brother. Edward smiled until he heard what Danny had to say next.

"You know what? Cassie said she was gonna go to her secret hideout tonight to get some stuff for us to play with!"

The brothers looked at each other.

"What was that . . . ?!"

"Wait, she doesn't mean . . ."

Thuh-kunk. There was a tremendously deep boom, and the clinic shook.

"Oh, no!"

Fearing the worst, Edward dashed outside. In the still driving rain, he could see several lanterns wobbling, moving toward the abandoned mine entrance toward Cassie's secret hideout.

Edward and Alphonse ran at top speed up the path to the mine entrance and pushed through the crowd of villagers.

The entrance, standing so sturdily earlier that day, had collapsed in half. The boards placed in an "X" had snapped in two, their splinters scattered on the rock-strewn ground under the driving rain.

Cassie's mother and father were there. From their expressions, and those of the people around them, it was clear that Cassie was inside.

"What happened? What happened?" Dr. Norm shouted from behind the brothers. He had followed them up the path.

One of the villagers turned, raising his lantern. "Someone heard Cassie calling for help from inside the mine, Doctor! Pitt went in after her . . . but before they came out, the cave collapsed!"

"Pitt's in there too?!" Alphonse shouted, growing increasingly worried. "What do we do, Ed?"

"That idiot!" Edward crouched down to touch the rocky side of the hill next to the mine entrance. Large stones had been piled here to reinforce the mine years ago, but they were loose now. They moved freely when Edward gave them a light push with his hand. Behind him, he could hear the anxious voices of the villagers.

"What do we do? And what was Cassie doing coming up here in the first place?"

"Pitt should have known better than to go in by himself! Now we've got two kids stuck in there . . ."

"It's not going to be easy getting them out!"

His back turned to the crowd, Edward lifted his lamp and peered through the wreckage of the mine entrance. "Cassie kept stuff in here—her treasures," he said without turning. "When she went in to get them, the cave must have collapsed and trapped her. Pitt came up here looking after his herbs, and . . ."

Edward stuck his head in through a gap in the rocks. In the gloom beyond the mess near the entrance he could see a narrow path angling down into the darkness. "It's not wide enough for an adult in there. That's why Pitt went in alone."

"Can you do something with your alchemy, Ed?" Alphonse

asked, but Edward looked out from the wreckage and shook his head.

"Not a chance. There's been a big cave-in, and I don't know the structure of the place well enough to begin with. I won't be able to do anything from the outside."

"Maybe we could dig in slowly . . . ?" One of the villagers came up and went to touch the gap in the rocks. Edward grabbed his hand, stopping him.

"If we just start digging blindly, we could bring down the rest of the tunnel."

"So what do we do?! Is there no way to help Cassie?!" her father shouted behind them. "While we sit out here discussing this, she could be . . . !"

Dr. Norm came up behind Cassie's parents and put a hand on each of their shoulders. "It's a little early to lose hope just yet."

"That's right," Edward agreed. "I can repair the collapsed sections here bit by bit, then work my way through that gap . . . " As he spoke, Edward took off his jacket. "If Pitt got in there, so can I."

Edward clapped his hands together, used a little alchemy to strengthen the rocks around the gap in the rubble, and began to crawl in. The passage was narrow, but if he twisted his body in just the right way he found he could keep moving forward. "I think I can make it. I'm going in."

"Be careful!"

Alphonse took the lamp from Dr. Norm and watched as his brother worked his way past the rubble. "Good luck, Ed!"

"Yep," Edward replied, looking around and waving his hand as best he could before heading down into the mine.

The slope leading in from the entrance had collapsed partially, leaving only about three feet of crawl space beneath it. Edward continued on, doubled over, tracing the rusted mining-cart rails with his feet, and gradually, the light from the villagers at the entrance grew dim until he could no longer see. Edward lifted his own lamp and lit it.

Gradually, the sound of the heavy rain outside grew distant, and silence wrapped around Edward.

"Things look better in here . . ." he muttered, looking around at the shaft. Unlike the entrance, the walls and ceiling here seemed to be mostly in their original condition. Protected from the elements, they hadn't weathered as much as parts of the mine closer to the surface. Edward continued down, pausing occasionally to fix a crumbling wall or ceiling rafter with his alchemy.

In a short while, he found himself in the mineshaft proper, and the tunnel became large enough for him to stand at full height. Lifting his lamp he looked around. The tunnel was now a proper mineshaft, with square corners, and it branched every now and then.

"Pitt! Cassie!" Edward shouted down each branching tunnel he came to, but no reply came, other than his own voice echoing in the darkness. "Great. Guess I'll just have to follow my gut."

Edward lifted his lamp higher, squinting his eyes at the darkness ahead. All around him stood nothing but earthen walls and the wooden beams that supported them. No Pitt, no Cassie. At least, he thought with some relief, the structure of the mine was sound down here. When they had heard the collapse from the clinic, he had feared the worst, yet it seemed that it had been more bark than bite.

Still, he hadn't heard a sign of Pitt and Cassie, and since they hadn't come out on their own, they must have gotten stuck under something.

Edward stopped at every intersection, looking long down each shaft, picking the ones that seemed to be in the worst condition before going on. "Pitt could at least have come to get me first . . ." Edward said out loud, trying to fend off the faint claustrophobia he felt walking down the mineshafts alone. With his alchemy, he could have come down to help get Cassie and avoided getting two of them trapped. But Pitt was angry at Edward, and when the emergency came, he wanted to fix it himself. That was Pitt's mistake.

"What's that guy's problem, anyway?" Edward said, scowling at the silent darkness.

Edward lightly brushed his fingers across his cheek. He could feel the swelling even through the poultice Dr. Norm had given him. Edward's brows furrowed. In the past, he had always known without thinking how Pitt would feel about something. But now, his old friend felt like a complete mystery to him. He couldn't understand why Pitt had hit him or why he had run down the mineshaft alone. "One thing's for sure—he was never like this before," Edward muttered angrily.

He'd been surprised at first to see how much Pitt had changed in the years since they last met. His one-time reckless co-conspirator was calm, even polite. A doctor in training. Edward had been impressed, so much that he regretted not having made more progress himself over the last year.

But now that he thought about it, something was wrong. Pitt seemed to be holding himself back—letting people complain to him without so much as a word in response. When he ran away from Cassie, who had only wanted him to make medicine, and when he hit Edward, he hadn't given any reason for his actions. The old Pitt never would have turned away without saying a word. And he would never have tried something as foolhardy as this.

Pitt had changed, but not all of it was good. "It's like he's a different person," Edward said, shuffling forward. His mind churned with questions.

At last he came to a place where the square tunnel warped and sagged. The ceiling here had collapsed, and part of the wall and the support beams were crumbling. There was a damp smell in the air. If he was looking for a place that had collapsed in the rain last night, this was looking like a candidate.

"Pitt! Cassie!" Edward shouted, then stopped to listen. Hearing no reply, he made his way deeper through the collapsed tunnel and repeated the process.

After he had done this several times, he thought he heard a faint sound in the darkness. He came to a stop and listened.

The tunnel was so quiet it made his ears ring, but then he heard it again—a sound like crumbling dirt coming from somewhere. Then, at regular intervals, he heard the sound of rocks rubbing against rocks. Somebody was picking up rocks, digging their way out.

Edward oriented himself toward the noise and began to run. He passed several intersections and kept going, fixing the shaft where he could, until he saw a faint light ahead. It was a lamp. Edward ran faster, making his way toward that lamp bobbing in the darkness ahead. "Pitt!"

Ahead, a lantern sat on the rocky floor of the mineshaft. Next to it, Pitt clawed away at a wall of rocks with all his might.

"You're okay!" Edward shouted, running up. "Where's Cassie?!" He stopped and looked up at the wall of rocks blocking the passageway. He had a lot of things on his mind to say, and he still hadn't forgotten about the punch he owed Pitt, but now hardly seemed like the time.

Pitt was working at a foot-wide hole in the rocks and earth. Peering through it, Edward could see Cassie lying asleep on the other side. "Is she hurt?"

"She's just tired herself out crying," Pitt responded without looking around. His hands kept moving, working at rocks.

"Right, I'll reinforce the tunnel around here and open a larger hole." Pitt was right, they had to dig through the rocks, but if they tried to move them without reinforcing the surrounding tunnel they could bring the whole place down on themselves.

Edward put his hands together, ready to start his alchemy, but Pitt knocked one of his hands away. "What are you doing?!" Edward yelled, but Pitt merely turned and continued clawing at the rocks. Edward frowned and slapped his hands together again, only to have Pitt knock them aside once more.

The blood rushed to Edward's head. He grabbed Pitt by the collar. "What's wrong with you? Are you crazy? Stop getting in the way!"

"I don't need your alchemy!" Pitt roared back, his yelling drowning out Edward's own. "I'll save Cassie! I don't need you here!" With a surge of strength, Pitt pushed Edward away and turned back to his stones. Edward stared at his back, his expression a mixture of disbelief and rage. "What's gotten into you? Are you trying to be some kind of hero? Can't you pick a time that's not an emergency to play?"

"Say what you want! I'm doing this, and I don't need your help!"

"Stop being stupid and step aside!" Edward scowled, grabbing Pitt by the shoulder and yanking him backward hard. "If you want to prove you can do something on your own, go make medicine! I heard you can make Danny's medicine after all! Go do that, and leave this to me!"

Pitt stumbled backward and fell to the ground. Edward didn't so much as glance behind him, slapping his hands together for a third time. He placed his palms on the wall as an alchemical light flared in the dim tunnel. The wall of the mineshaft gradually transformed, becoming harder, stronger. The crumbling earthen wall transformed into a hard, shiny surface that spread to cover all the rocks around the hole Pitt had made. The rocks melded with each other to form one solid rock wall.

Edward brought his hands together again, touching the new rock wall in front of him. When the light faded, a hole had formed in the wall large enough for a child to crawl through.

"Cassie!" Edward went through to the other side and picked the girl up in his arms. Cassie held a collection of pretty stones and beetle cages in her hands—the collection she had meant to show Danny. Even asleep, exhausted, she clung to her precious treasures. Traces of tears glistened on her cheeks, washing clean lines into her dirt-covered face, but dirty though she was, she did not seem injured. Edward breathed a sigh of relief and carried Cassie back through the hole in the wall.

There he found Pitt, both hands on the ground, his head slumped low. "Why did you have to come in here?" he asked, his voice barely a whisper.

Edward raised an eyebrow. "Why? I came to help you and Cassie," he replied coldly, still unable to fathom Pitt's inexplicable attitude.

All his thoughts of getting payback had disappeared,

overcome by his earlier regret that he didn't understand his old friend anymore.

"Came to help?" Pitt raised his head, looking up at Edward. He looked as though he were in pain. "You say that so easily . . . you do it so easily . . . how come you can do that all by yourself? How come you get to be someone? How do I get to be someone?!"

"Get to be someone?" Edward echoed back, startled. "You *are* someone! Not me." Edward furrowed his brow, then spoke again, this time more softly, with a hint of regret in his voice. "I knew you'd changed when I first saw you, and I thought it was for the best. Just a year out of Resembool and you were already a full-fledged assistant. But you've changed so much . . . You're not Pitt anymore."

In part, Edward worried that the change he saw in Pitt was only a sign of how little he himself had changed in the last year. His friend was pulling ahead, and he couldn't keep up. That year had put space between them, a gap that couldn't be crossed easily. Edward grew sad thinking about it.

But Pitt shook his head. "I'm not anyone! I know I'm not myself . . . I know that much. But I . . . but I have to change . . . I have to do something!" Pitt's voice echoed through the mine. "What was that you said about Danny's medicine? Yeah, I can make it. They just won't let me!"

"Won't let you?" Edward furrowed his brow again at the unexpected words. He had assumed there was another more practical reason why Pitt was unable to make his medicine—be it a lack of the right herbs of something else. It never occurred to him that someone might be stopping Pitt from making the medicine Danny needed. "Why not?"

Pitt's medicine was effective, and cheap to make. He couldn't see why anyone wouldn't want it—Cassie had practically begged him to make it. Pitt's shoulders slouched even deeper. "I made a mistake one time—a misdiagnosis. They don't trust me anymore."

"A mistake?"

". . . It was about half a year after I came here. Danny had a cold. I thought it was just a regular cough. I wasn't supposed to do anything without the doctor there, but his parents told me they wanted medicine, anything would do, so I gave them some herbal remedies I'd made. I was careful to pick only the mildest ones, ones that couldn't possibly harm anyone, but he had an allergic reaction . . ."

Pitt scratched at the ground, reliving his humiliation and regret at the failure.

Edward remembered seeing how Danny's mother ignored Pitt at the clinic, how Danny's father had been so cold to him. "I get it, so that's why you . . ."

Pitt had backed down in the clinic and on the bridge in the rain because he knew he had been wrong. That's why he wasn't acting like the Pitt that Edward knew. It wasn't hard to imagine the Rymars pressuring Pitt into giving the medicine, either.

But none of them had known about Danny's allergy, clearly. It had been an honest mistake, and a forgivable one, but ill feelings festered between the Rymars and Pitt. Danny's parents had lost their faith in anything but the most expensive, strongest medication. When Cassie asked Pitt to make more for Danny, she must not have known what had happened.

It must have been tough for Pitt, wanting only to help yet being denied by Danny's parents, unable to honor Cassie's request. So he pretended to be someone else in order to hide the pain, the irritation, the unhappiness. He pretended to be an adult, unflappable and emotionless.

Pitt sat up with his back to one of the walls and moved a hand over his face to fix his glasses. "I can't do anything. I'm just a kid. Once, it got to be too much for me, and I even ran back to Resembool. But you left and never looked back, didn't you? Your alchemy's as good as your teacher's, even!"

Pitt kept his hand over his face. "We used to be even. But somehow, you pulled ahead and left me behind! I didn't want to lose. That's why I left Resembool after you—but now, I see you again a year later, and you're so far ahead of me . . ." A single tear fell from beneath the rim of Pitt's glasses.

Edward noticed for the first time that whenever Pitt had paused to fix his glasses, it was to hide the pain in his face or the tears in his eyes. At last, he finally understood that while Pitt had seemed so far ahead of him, Pitt had thought the same thing of Edward.

"Come on . . ." Edward stood next to Pitt, reaching out

a hand. "Stop trying to crank up the pressure on me to get ahead. Let's go."

"What? I thought I just told you, I was the one worried about falling behind . . ."

Pitt stared suspiciously at Edward's outstretched hand. Edward grinned.

The two boys really were a lot alike.

In height, temperament—especially their stubbornness—and the way they both tried too hard to be first, they were exactly the same.

Pitt had wanted to go get the medicine in the rain and had come to save Cassie because he wanted to be someone people could trust more than anything else. Edward wanted to find the Philosopher's Stone and get back what he and his brother had lost more than anything else. Both of them wanted to move forward, and both looked at each other and worried the other would succeed first.

Dr. Norm had probably realized that the two boys were mirror images of each other. That's why he had known exactly the right advice to give to Edward—because he knew Pitt. Both of them needed to learn how to take it easy.

Edward realized he had been holding his breath. He let it out in a long, quiet sigh. "You know, when I saw you again the other day, I felt certain you were the one who'd moved ahead."

"Huh?" Pitt looked up in surprise.

"We were neck and neck back in Resembool. But here I thought you had gone and left me behind. It was hard for me to see you working at the clinic, looking so successful, hard for me to know I didn't have a home to go back to. I thought about a lot of stuff."

Pitt listened silently.

"The thing is, we both chose paths that would lead us to adulthood faster than any of our friends. We have to be ready to deal with pressure—grown-up pressure. You know, to be adult."

Edward no longer worried about getting ahead.

He knew there would be trouble enough in the days and months to come. He just had to meet it without comparing himself to anyone. He would face whatever challenges waited for him on his own terms, as would Edward.

Edward laughed, but Pitt didn't take his hand.

"Whatever," Pitt mumbled, and before Edward could move, Pitt swiped up with his own hand, connecting with Edward's palm in a painful high five. Pitt grinned.

It was the same grin as always, the same old Pitt.

THE NEXT MORNING, three figures stood on a hill over the village. A refreshing breeze blew, and the sky looked clear blue, without a single shred of cloud, as though the heavy rains of the night before had been only a dream.

"All right! The rain's stopped, the wind is good—a perfect day to restart our journey!" Edward said with a loud yawn, sucking in as much of the crisp air as he could. Pitt stood next to him, waiting to see the brothers off. Now he pointed toward a mountain in the distance.

"There's a large town over that way. Should be a train station there, too."

"Right, thanks!"

"Thanks for everything, Pitt. And give our regards to Dr. Norm and the other people in town."

"Sure thing."

In his arms, Alphonse carried a bag stuffed with fruit pancakes. The villagers had come out and showered them with gifts when they tried to leave, both in thanks for building the new dykes on the river, and for saving Cassie. Dr. Norm threw in some antibacterial bandages, and Cassie gave them a card.

Edward reached out, plucking the card from the bag and opened it quietly.

Inside, she had drawn a picture of Danny and Cassie and their parents holding hands, with a caption that read "Thanks, Edward and Alphonse!"

"Looks like Cassie's going to be fine."

"Yeah."

Edward and Alphonse looked down the hill toward the village. The water from the heavy rains had begun to drain from the fields, and here and there, tiny waves rippled across the remaining large puddles.

The river flowed gently once again, and children played around the new reservoir. Unable to catch bugs now that all the tall grasses by the riverbank had been swept away, the kids had quickly shifted gears to fishing. Edward and Alphonse spotted Cassie among the group of kids with fishing poles over their shoulders laughing as they cast their lines. Danny was sitting next to her.

After they had learned why their daughter was going into the mines, and after a word of advice from Dr. Norm, Cassie's parents were trying to let Danny and Cassie play together as much as possible. The best thing for Danny was not to be too overprotective of him and to let him build his strength. Besides, if Cassie could help her parents look after her brother, it would strengthen her bond with them at the same time.

Even when they left the water's edge and ran around, Cassie always kept an eye on her little brother. Only one day in, and she already filled the role of big sister perfectly.

"I hope you can fix those bad vibes between you and the Rymars soon too," Edward said.

Pitt shook his head lightly. "It's hard to gain somebody's trust once you've lost it. The best I can hope for is to not make another mistake the next time they ask for something," Pitt responded calmly, taking off his glasses. "Guess I need to study some more."

It wasn't an offhand comment. Pitt had thought things through. He was ready to face reality. His face looked relaxed, brighter, as though the demons that plagued him had finally called off their attack.

"You look more like the old Pitt without the glasses." Edward watched his friend squinting in the light.

"You think?"

"Yeah."

Pitt had never worn glasses in Resembool. Edward and Alphonse were used to seeing his face when he wasn't hiding behind a pair of lenses. Those familiar mischievous brown eyes twinkled.

Pitt handed Edward his glasses. "Try them on."

"Me? But I don't wear glasses. It will be all blurry." Still, Edward set down his traveling trunk, put on Pitt's glasses, and stared out across the field. "See . . . Huh?" The field looked exactly the same as it had before he put the glasses on. "Wait . . . These aren't real? They're just glass?" Edward tried taking the glasses off and putting them back on several times until he was convinced that the lenses weren't lenses at all.

"Yeah," Pitt said with a smile. "I got sick of people calling me a kid, so I wanted to spruce up my image a bit. But, like you said, there's no point in rushing to grow up, is there? I guess I don't need those anymore."

"Heh," Edward laughed, knowing all too well how his friend felt.

It was part of a young boy's nature to want to grow up as fast as he could, and it was the silliest thing to do. Edward and Pitt had finally realized that they could only keep walking forward, at their own pace. There was no point in hurrying, and there were no shortcuts.

Edward toyed with the glasses a bit, then put them on again and turned to Pitt and Alphonse. "What do you think, are they me?" Edward asked with a grin.

The two shook their heads immediately. "No way."

"C'mon, you can lie just a little. Say I look grown-up!"

"Not even a little."

"You'll always be a kid, Edward, you know that."

"Whaaaat?!"

Alphonse and Pitt laughed, running away from Edward's raised fist. For a while they chased each other through the grass like they had so many times before. It took Pitt several minutes to get his laughter under control. "Hey, remember when I said I had gone back to Resembool once?"

"Yeah?"

"Well, I went to Winry's house. What do you think she was doing?"

Edward, taken aback at the sudden mention of his old friend, shrugged as casually as he could. "Probably working on some Auto-Mail like always?"

"Winry always did love the stuff."

Edward, Alphonse, and Pitt all knew of Winry's disdain for "girly" things. Her one love had always been for tinkering with Auto-Mail.

Pitt shook his head slowly. "Wrong. Pinako was teaching her how to cook stew!"

"Winry was cooking?!"

Pitt had gone back to Resembool the day after he had made his misdiagnosis of Danny's cough. When he walked by the Rockbell house, he had caught a whiff of stew coming from the kitchen and looked in to see Winry toiling over a giant pot on the stove.

"Of course, she's still working on Auto-Mail too—gotten quite good from what I heard. But there she was, making stew for dinner. Even Pinako seemed surprised that she wanted to learn. She asked me if I knew anyone who liked stew . . ." Pitt grinned at Edward and Alphonse. "You two are big stew fans, aren't you?"

"Yes, we both love stew," Alphonse happily admitted.

Alphonse was happy to hear that Winry hadn't forgotten their favorite food even after they'd been gone more than a year. Edward sat quietly by his brother.

"You were saying you didn't have a home to go back to, but I bet I know someone in Resembool who would feed you and put a roof over your heads if you dropped by."

Pitt's words reminded Edward of what he'd said to Cassie, when she didn't want to go home. He cast his eyes downward, watching the grass by his feet waver in the soft breeze.

We can't go home. We don't have a home to go back to.

What if they see what little progress I've made in the year. I don't want them to worry.

What if I went back and didn't want to leave again.

That's why he hadn't even called his friends in Resembool. He hadn't written. He hadn't gone home. Yet all that seemed to be melting away now.

"Maybe you're right . . ."

Families. They welcomed you home and gave you something warm to eat. That's what families do. Edward realized how important that seemingly simple thing was and how much he and his brother had longed for it. Without effort, without even trying, families made you feel like you belonged. Without knowing it, this was what Winry had wanted. She longed to make them feel that, when they came to Resembool, they would be coming home.

Edward had the feeling that, if they came stumbling back into town, still bearing the heavy burden of fate on their backs, Winry would greet them as though they had just come back from a day playing outside. That's how she was. She would give them the same welcome if they decided they never wanted to leave again or if they couldn't wait to get back on the road. It came as a deep relief to Edward to know there was a place—and a person—like that left in the world.

Pitt placed his hand on Edward's shoulder. "You might not have your own house to go back to, but you always have a home. There are people waiting for you. Don't forget them."

Though he hadn't told Edward, when Pitt went back to Resembool, he had learned two things. The first was that the person he longed to see again most was Winry, and the reason he had always picked on her so much was because he had a crush on her.

The second thing he learned was that she had devoted herself to honing her skills—first Auto-Mail and now stew—all for the sake of the boy who had lived next door, and she didn't have so much as a thought for Pitt. Unable to confess to Edward how he had realized his first love and lost her at the same time, he did the next best thing and hit him on the shoulder. Hard.

"Owch!"

"Go get 'em, Edward!" Pitt grinned, hitting Edward again.

Edward, oblivious to the thoughts going through Pitt's head, stuck his arm out in front of him. "We're heading out."

"See ya."

Pitt put his own arm out to meet Edward's, a challenge in his smile. "Next time we meet up, let's see which one of us is closer to reaching his goal. And I warn you, I hate losing."

The backs of their arms met in front of their faces. It was a tradition—whenever they made up from a fight or came up with a particularly naughty plan, they would hit their arms together like this—wishing each the best of luck and at the same time each vowing that he would be the winner.

"Later!"

"Thanks, Pitt!"

"You too, Alphonse!"

And so the three parted on the hill, to each their own path. Pitt went back down into the village, and Edward and Alphonse turned to begin the next step of their journey.

But, only a few moments later, Pitt's voice rang out across the hill. "Heeeey!"

The brothers turned to see Pitt waving from a considerable distance.

Edward and Alphonse waved back, thinking this was his final send-off, when they saw a small object flying through the air toward them. At the same time, Pitt's voice reached them on the wind.

"Beat you by half an inch!"

Edward picked up the object which had fallen in the grass by their feet, to find it was a small bottle. He read the label.

"P-paint thinner? What's this?!"

"Ack!" Alphonse twisted his head around to look at his own back. Two marks had been painted on his back in red paint, one a full half-inch above the other. Next to that was painted the words "I win."

"What the heck?"

"It's your and Pitt's heights. I don't know why he thinks he can use me as a measuring post . . ." Alphonse sighed.

Edward stared at his brother's back. "Heights? Wait, so what does that mean?! This mark below, is that supposed to be me or something? So that means I'm shorter than he is?!"

"I guess that's what it's supposed to mean."

"Pitt! No way am I accepting this as evidence! I never agreed to any of this!"

Edward turned around, gritting his teeth, but Pitt was nowhere to be seen.

He knew his friend well enough to know where he was going. By now he would be heading back to his desk to study. Once he'd taken on a challenge, he didn't mean to lose.

Edward turned, impatient to get on with his own task and began to walk.

The gentle breeze blew against his face. Edward brushed back his bangs.

"Hey, Ed," Alphonse called out as they began to walk.

"Hmm?"

"Let's make a stop by Resembool someday soon . . . if we happen to be in the area."

"Yeah, let's," Edward replied, as though it were the most natural thing in the world. "I would like to see how Pinako and Winry are doing, if only for a day or two . . . but we can't *really* go home until . . ."

"Until we have our bodies back, right?" Alphonse said with a laugh, finishing his brother's sentence for him.

"That's right!"

He didn't know how long it would take them to reach their goal, but he had to keep moving forward. And what better reason than that for stopping to take a break sometimes? Just knowing there were people waiting for them took a little of the weight off his shoulders, and strengthened his resolve all the more. "Hope you're ready for this next leg of the trip, Al—got a feeling it's going to be a long one!"

"You bet!"

Edward and Alphonse stepped back onto the road beneath a sky far from home.

Story Two

Roy's Vacation

IT WAS ANOTHER day of work at Eastern Command when Roy opened the documents from Captain Hawkeye and his face, weary from many late nights of work, twisted into a frown.

"I knew the orders would come some day, I was just kind of hoping it wouldn't be today."

Roy Mustang was a military man in the unwelcome position of possessing two duties: one as a state alchemist, the other as ranking officer at Eastern Command. Though the dark locks of hair that fell over his forehead made him look boyish at times, he had talent enough to make him a colonel at an unprecedented young age, and though he had made many enemies, his peers always held him in high esteem.

The orders he referred to were for a bit of training. If you belong to the military, particular duty required that, once every several years, you be assigned to go for extensive training sessions. The frequency and content of these sessions varied by rank. Some people found themselves spending a week listening to lecture after lecture in the halls of Central, while others were sent to work under an officer at a different command.

Roy's orders were neither of these. He was to go to a command center well off the beaten path. He would polish his skills as a commanding officer in unfamiliar territory, and hopefully do some polishing of the local troops along the way.

Either way, it meant a long trip, a disruption in his daily lifestyle, and ordering around people he'd never met. Training orders never thrilled anyone—most people accepted them only begrudgingly. Roy's sour expression showed he was no exception.

In one corner of the bustling room, Roy paused in his desk work and sighed. "I can't believe they're sending me way out there . . ." His assigned destination was so far away from Eastern Command that it raised doubts as to why a base had been built there in the first place.

"You aren't seriously considering going?" one of his subordinates sitting nearby asked incredulously.

"I don't have a choice," he replied. "Can't refuse an order from Central." Roy looked up at Captain Hawkeye standing in front of his desk, still waiting for his response.

"I'll do my job as a soldier . . . tell them that."

"Understood. The commanding officer from one of the other branches will be taking your place here in the interim, Colonel. I'll need you to get on those transfer documents as soon as possible."

"Fine. I'll be working in the officer's room, if you need me."

"Wait!"

Just as Roy was starting to stand, a crowd of men swarmed up to his desk, each jostling to be first in line. It was second lieutenants Breda and Havoc, Warrant Officer Falman, and Master Sergeant Fuery.

"You can't leave that giant pile of work behind!"

"If you're really going, at least write an opinion for that weapons development proposal I gave you. It's been on your desk for ten days now, and you haven't written a word!"

"What about those materials I loaned you a week ago? I'll need those back soon . . ."

"Please, before you go, sign the reports from our meetings with the other branches, please! I gave them to you two weeks ago! They're already way past deadline for submission to Central!"

Roy quietly shook his head. "I'm sorry, but my training orders have come through, and it's my duty to go. Believe me, it's hard for me to leave all this work in your hands. Please understand." A sincere look on his face, Roy clapped each man on the shoulder in turn. "Look, anything I haven't done, I'll do as soon as I get back!"

"That's what you always say, but you never do it!" Breda grumbled. If they'd learned anything during their service at Eastern Command, Roy's subordinates knew never to trust a promise to do work from their colonel.

Roy was short-tempered, quick to take action, and swift

at decision-making, yet when it came to desk work, slugs moved faster.

Fuery tugged on his arm. "Just sign them, please!"

"All I want is my materials back."

"You can't leave, I still got three stacks for you to look at!"

Roy waved one arm in a sweeping gesture. "Enough! Can't you see I'm too busy to deal with these . . . clerical things?" Roy brushed off their clinging hands and, carrying his training orders, retreated into the officer's room.

The door shut behind him with a slam, and there was the sound of a lock turning.

Roy let out a long sigh of relief, alone at last. After a moment to calm himself, he held up the letter in his hand and looked at it again. Roy grabbed the files and documents occupying his desk and shoved them into a drawer. Then, from the same drawer, he pulled out a map and spread it in the newly created space on his desk.

"Not bad. Not bad at all," Roy said with a chuckle, his frown loosening and eventually curling upward into a smile.

His destination, though provincial, was far from the border, which meant far from any real danger. It was a tiny town, surrounded by wilderness. There would be nothing for the military to do there.

This suited Roy perfectly.

If all went well, he could probably get away without doing any training either. By the time they were formally part of the military, all soldiers had been through boot camp. Why would they need anything more than that?

In fact, this training was beginning to look more and more like a vacation. No more long, hard days working like a dog at Eastern Command, having his subordinates shout at him, pressuring him about deadlines and paperwork. Sure, he had a responsibility to his men, but even colonels need to take a break sometimes.

He had realized this from the moment the orders came, of course. Fortunately, he had mastered the art of feigning disappointment.

"I think it's time for a hard-earned vacation." Grinning to himself, Roy spent the rest of the week counting off the days till his departure.

THINGS HAVE A WAY of never going as smoothly as planned. Everything went fine as Roy handled the transfer of authority to the interim commanding officer. He waved good-bye to his subordinates, who came running after him all the way to the station, piles of papers awaiting his signature stacked high in their hands. Everything kept going fine until, after a long train ride, he arrived at his destination in the middle of the biggest rainstorm in years. The convoy sent to greet him was an hour late, by which time the rain had thoroughly soaked Roy and all his baggage. When he asked the reason for the delay, the driver nervously explained that a flock of sheep had been blocking the road. They hadn't been able to get through.

FULLMETAL ALCHEMIST

Roy had expected to find himself in the peaceful country-side. He just hadn't expected it to be quite *this* peaceful.

Once on base, Roy looked at his schedule only to find nothing written on it at all. When he asked why, the sergeant on duty explained that there had been nothing to write. Normal duties for the base included fixing broken bridges, chasing runaway cows, and helping organize local festivals. When Roy wondered out loud what the point of keeping a schedule was if no one used it, a sergeant helpfully went up to the board and wrote, in the blank space for that day: "No activity planned on account of heavy rain."

Scratching his head, Roy went to examine the base munitions and found the door unlocked. Everything inside was covered with an inch of dust, and birds had built a nest on one of the rifle crates. Fearing that the soldiers here might have forgotten how to use their weapons entirely, Roy sent out a call for all soldiers who weren't otherwise occupied to draw their holstered sidearms for an inspection.

It turned out that only half of them were armed at all, and only a handful of them had actually loaded their weapons. Worse, when he counted the assembled soldiers he realized with a start that he was looking at the entire base. He had asked for soldiers who weren't occupied, and got everyone. Even the men on guard duty and the communications officer, who was expressly forbidden to leave his post.

Roy was not impressed. Shouting at the top of his lungs, he soon found himself far from enjoying a pleasant vacation in the countryside—and busier than he had ever been at Eastern Command retraining the troops.

FOR SIX DAYS, Roy ran around, barking orders until he was hoarse. He nurtured his twentieth headache of the morning as he prepared for an emergency simulation drill.

"Lord Colonel! I wrote up a plan for the training, I was wondering if you could check it? I wasn't entirely sure if I got everything right . . ."

"Lord Colonel, am I holding my gun correctly? Oh, and when you tell us to assemble with our weapons, which weapons did you mean, exactly?"

Sergeants Natts and Cayt stood before him, asking question after question, utterly oblivious to how ridiculous they sounded. If it weren't for the serious looks on their faces, Roy would have thought they were joking with him.

Natts gripped the training plan in one white-knuckled hand. His large, dark eyes stared at Roy from beneath a neatly trimmed brown forelock. He was the son of a shepherd in town, who seemed most at ease when he was moving and talking slowly, yet after seeing the fullness of Roy's wrath six days ago, his voice had gone up a full octave, and everything he did, he did with the desperation that comes from trying to avoid having wrath coming down on him.

Next to him stood Cayt, squinting his brown eyes beneath a shock of blond hair as he fixed his grip on his rifle. He was a year older than the other soldier, but both were still barely old enough to grow whiskers on their chins. The other soldiers claimed Sergeant Cayt had the happiest disposition of anyone on base, but even he withered before Roy's glare. He had glanced nervously back between his rifle and the colonel no fewer than forty-seven times since entering the room.

Roy looked across the desk in at the two young sergeants and sighed.

"Whatever happened to that vacation . . ."

"Excuse me, sir?" Cayt asked, leaning forward and putting a hand to one ear to hear his mumbling. Roy glared at them both. "The plans are all wrong. And you're holding your rifle wrong, too. Why can't you folks perform even the simplest tasks here? And don't ask me about every little thing. Try putting yourself in my shoes, having to answer the same inane questions over and over."

"S-sorry, sir!"

"Our apologies, Lord Colonel!"

The two saluted, looking truly chagrined, and Roy's heart sank. Now he felt like a bully.

"I need a break," he muttered, when there was a quick knock at the door.

"Come in," Roy growled. He found himself wondering which basic question or which failure report he was about to be subjected to.

Yet the first sound he heard from behind the opening door was a deep belly laugh.

"Hey, how're you doing?"

Roy's expression transformed from a cold glare to wide-eyed surprise. In front of the open door stood the last two people in the world he had expected to see. "Lieutenant Colonel Hughes and Major Armstrong?!"

"Well, you look all the worse for wear! I see the rumors are true—they've finally put the ever-unflappable Colonel Mustang to work!" It was Maes Hughes. The laughter had been his.

Hughes, with his short cropped black hair and trademark square-rimmed glasses, was a military man to the core, much like Roy. He was as smart as they came, yet he always seemed to be laughing at some private joke. He never ran out of biting wit when his friend Roy was the subject. Even now, though he sympathized for the obviously harried Roy, he couldn't help but seem immensely pleased.

"Why the sudden arrival? I didn't receive any word about this visit!" Roy blustered.

Armstrong stepped forward and gave a crisp salute. "It's been a long time, Colonel Mustang. As for our sudden appearance, we did send word via wireless before leaving, I assure you."

Armstrong carried himself with a refined, dignified air. He wore a well-groomed golden beard and moustache beneath his round, kind eyes. A major in the army, he, like Roy, possessed the title of state alchemist. He was a caring, cautious sort, with a warm character, but the most impressive thing about him was his sheer physical mass. He stood so tall he practically touched the ceiling, and every inch of his massive frame was covered with muscle, making the spacious room seem almost cramped. "We informed your communications officer to advise you of our imminent arrival. Perhaps there was some mistake? Hmm? Colonel? Are you feeling ill?" said Armstrong, tilting his head.

Roy's head fell forward and his forehead slammed into his desk with a resounding *thunk*. "How many times did I tell him he needed to make those reports!"

"Lord Colonel! We'll have a word with the communications officer at once!" Sergeant Natts shouted eagerly.

"Leave it to us, sir!" Sergeant Cayt chimed in.

"Look," Roy sighed. "Drop the 'Lord,' and instead of worrying about other people's jobs, work on getting yours straight first. We'll hold off on the emergency situation training until later. Go back over your plans again before then. And you— make sure you know how to wield and present those arms. Dismissed!" Roy's head still pressed to the desk, he waved his hand to dismiss sergeants Natts and Cayt from the room.

"Yes, sir!"

"Sorry, sir!"

Their shoulders slumping, the two young sergeants shuffled out the door.

The moment the door slam shut, Roy's head jerked up from his desk. "I can't take it anymore! Let's go get a drink!"

Hughes laughed uproariously, and Armstrong chuckled beside him.

"Things must really be bad. I've never seen you look so

down," Hughes remarked, going over to stand by the window where he could look down on the soldiers running through their drills in the courtyard below. They were apparently attempting to run in single file, but from above they looked more like a drunken snake. The cause of Roy's despair was clear.

"I'm fine with going to get a drink. We just reached a break in our work anyway."

"You had work to do? Out in this backwater?"

Hughes fingered his shirt, showing it to Roy. "Just the usual investigation detail. That's why we're dressed like this." By which he meant civilian clothes, as opposed to uniforms.

This sort of investigation was common. Most revolved around reports of people trying to overthrow the government or engaging in other subversive activities. Investigations were always carried out incognito, to avoid causing a stir among average citizens and tipping off truly dangerous people.

Basic inquiries came first, but when dangerous elements were found, they would call in the army to come clean things up. This enabled them to catch and quench potential fires early on, as well as send a message that if you stood against the army or planned acts of terrorism, you *were* being watched.

Hughes and Armstrong were on their way home from one such investigation.

"It was a contract renewal for a weapons factory. Everything looked to be going smoothly until a competitor's owner contacted our people, wondering whether we really wanted to keep a contract with a place that was hiding weapons from the military. Word was, these weapons had been hidden near a town not far from here."

Though the war was officially over, small conflicts and terrorism meant that weapons orders were ever on the rise. Weapons manufacturers could do worse than take the military as a client. Factories competed to get contracts, and it was a common thing for one factory to squeal on another's shortcomings in an attempt to get an edge over the competition.

The charge in this case was serious. If a factory contracted to make weapons for the military was making even better weaponry and keeping it hidden, possibly even selling to another buyer, that would be a huge problem. Dangerous weapons in the hands of terrorists and separatists was bad news for the state.

As it turned out, the lion's share of these inquiries were little more than wild goose chases. As a rule the assignments went to men of low rank. If there existed a shred of truth to these rumors, however, a thorough investigation was required. And this was how Lieutenant Commander Hughes ended up on the job.

"So did you find what you were looking for?"

Hughes and Armstrong shrugged simultaneously.

"It was nothing, as always. We went to the village to find that the village itself had been abandoned . . ."

"So, we figured after coming all the way out here for nothing we might as well stop and see your tired, old mug."

"I'm the consolation prize, am I? Great," Roy scowled.

Hughes laughed out loud. "Easy there, Colonel! Don't worry, we'll help you unwind. In fact, I have the perfect suggestion."

"What's that?"

"How about we head out for a little hike? I got a lead on a place with great views when we were pounding the pavement in a town near here. What do you think, Major?"

"Huh? Scenic location?"

"Ah, it seems the major wasn't listening. It's supposed to be near here, up on a hill. Clean air and a great view. It's still morning. We could probably get out there and back by noon."

Hughes stood up, all ready to go. Producing a map, he began to pore over it with Armstrong looking over his shoulder.

Roy was hesitant. Unlikely though it might be, the thought of something happening while he went off for a sightseeing tour sent shivers down his spine. He could already imagine his two young sergeants running around in a panic, looking for him. "Uh . . . I don't think I can leave for a whole half-day. Why don't we just go to the next town over after hours?"

Hughes clapped a hand on Roy's back. "What? It'll be fine! Nothing will happen. Did you know your base here has a perfect record? Not one incident since it was built! Hah! You need to take it easy, you know that? Just think of it as a vacation!"

"Vacation . . ." Roy couldn't hide the way the word made

his eyes shine. "You're right. Nothing will happen, will it? I should take a break!"

"That's what I'm saying! Now, go change into your civvies. Can't have officers romping through the hills during work hours!"

"And you won't feel like you're really taking a vacation in that uniform!"

Happy for the first time in weeks, Roy changed clothes and cleaned up the books and papers spread across his desk. Armstrong opened the door and called out to a soldier walking by.

"Excuse me, but we're borrowing the colonel here for the morning. It's a matter from Central, er . . ."

"Observations," Hughes chimed in. "We have orders to do some observations. Just do everything by the book while your commanding officer's away, got it? Good!"

"Book?" the man stammered.

"Right here!" Roy grinned as he slapped a thick manual in the flustered soldier's hands. "Think of this as training for an emergency situation, got it? Good luck, soldier!" With that, he left the still unsure man behind him and trotted off. "If you want a vacation, you have to seize the opportunity!"

"That's right. And after coming this far, I can't go back home without a good tale to tell my daughter!"

The two officers looked at each other and smiled, looking for all the world like two students playing hooky. Behind them, Armstrong chuckled, shaking his head. "Boys, boys . . ."

The three opened the base gates (made out of leftover

fencing from a nearby sheep ranch) and stepped out onto the road.

"Great morning for a hike!" Roy said, feeling free for the first time in a long time, when he heard a surprised voice behind them.

"Eh?!"

He turned around to see sergeants Natts and Cayt standing just inside the gate. "We had some questions, and we heard you were leaving," Natts said, pausing between each word to catch his breath. "But what's this about hiking? I thought you were leaving to make observations . . ."

Roy scratched his neck and grinned sheepishly. "Well, uh . . ."

Once again, Hughes came through with the follow-up. "It *is* observations. But it's, er, top-secret. So we gave it a code name! Operation: Hiking!"

"Oh!" Natts and Cayt nodded vigorously.

Roy was still uneasy. If word got out that he had gone hiking, and one of his superiors heard it, it would be reflected on his report. He looked at Hughes and immediately the other officer understood.

Together, they walked back through the gate and grabbed the two young sergeants by the shoulders. "I'm afraid you're going to have to come with us! Quick, get into some civilian clothes."

"Today, you've been promoted to investigators!"

"Really?!"

The thought of a secret assignment wiped away the chagrin

from being chewed out by Roy not less than thirty minutes ago, and their eyes sparkled with enthusiasm.

"Th-thank you, sir! Thank you!"

"We'll do our best, sir!"

"I expect nothing less!" Roy beamed, though inside, his stomach was churning. *The things I do for a little vacation.* Still, there was a bright side: a little interaction with their commanding officer off base might help relax the two young sergeants a little. *Heaven knows they need it!*

Roy waited for the two sergeants to change into their civilian clothes, and looked up. The sky stretched far over pastures where sheep and cows grazed, and the morning sun hung bright over the ridgeline to the east.

He was getting away from work, if only for half a day.

Roy smiled, fully prepared to enjoy this little slice of vacation for all it was worth.

LIFE SUCKS . . .

Several hours had passed since they left base. Roy stood, his smile frozen on his face.

Before his eyes towered a wall of rock. Here and there tufts of grass peaked through crevices in the rugged cliff face. Roy glared at the wall as though its presence in his path were a personal affront rather than an innocent act of topography. It was just one of many such rises they had scaled since their "leisurely hike" had begun.

"Exactly what about this is a 'hill'?!" Roy gasped between ragged breaths. A short distance ahead of him, Hughes looked back and gave him a thumbs-up.

"Secret mission! I couldn't come out and reveal we were actually going to a mountain!"

Roy considered retorting. Realizing it would only tire him out even more, he instead reached out and grabbed onto Hughes's extended thumb as hard as he could.

"Ouch! That hurts! Sorry, okay? I'm sorry! But I really did want to do something to change your mood!"

"This is supposed to change my mood? I thought you said this was supposed to be a light hike, not some death-defying mountaineering expedition!"

Roy wiped the sweat off his brow with one hand and looked up. The sun had already climbed high in the sky. Hughes's scenic spot supposedly lay somewhere at the top of this mountain—this impassable, unassailable peak. They scrabbled at the steep hillside, using both hands to work their way up, the close contact with the rain-sodden ground leaving them all caked with mud.

In the lead, Armstrong used his much-famed strength and muscles to their full extent, pulling up the lagging Natts and Cayt and guiding Roy and Hughes to the more manageable rocks and footholds. If not for his help, they all would have given up some time ago.

They had slipped countless times and scraped and bruised

themselves on thorny bushes and bare rock. By linking hands, they pulled and tugged until all five of them were out of breath. Finally, they reached a clearing on a woody section of hillside where they could rest.

"It'll be near evening by the time we reach the top. Maybe we should have tried going up the other side," Armstrong said, unfolding his map of the area to determine their position. The contour lines on the map clearly showed that this steep cliff led to a rather gentle descent on the other side.

Of course, going around to the other side meant returning to town and getting on a train. It would take them half a day just to reach the trail base—and despite all that, it was still probably quicker than trying to go up this shorter, more treacherous route.

"We should've gone around," Roy spat.

Hughes shook his head. "No, if I spend too much time tromping around these mountains, then that's time I won't have to spend with Alicia, isn't it?"

It was well known in military circles that Hughes was utterly devoted to his daughter, Alicia. Roy opened his mouth to complain.

"*Wooooooo . . .*"

Roy jerked up, for a second thinking that the low moaning sound had come from his own mouth. The low, growling rumble sounded like the howl of some beast. The other four, sitting exhausted upon the ground perked up their ears. They had all heard it.

The five hunkered together and peered into the dense undergrowth ahead of them, leaning ever-so-slightly toward each other, as though physical proximity would save them from whatever terror they had found. Vines grew thick on the trees ahead, forming a veritable wall of vegetation. The sound came from somewhere within that wall.

"You bring your sidearms?" Roy asked in a small voice, his gaze never wavering from the bushes.

Everyone nodded. Still, there was no guarantee that whatever made that sound could be taken down with pistols, and running didn't seem like the best option on this steep, treacherous slope. They would more likely than not end up tumbling to their deaths.

A light breeze blew against the tensed cheeks and jaw lines of the hiking party. They heard the sound again, a guttural growl that crept around them, resonating as though it were part of the rocks beneath their feet. Whatever made that noise was big. Really big.

"What the heck . . ." Roy shook his head, feeling the need to act like the ranking officer he was, yet not knowing what to do when Natts and Cayt tugged on his sleeve.

"Lord Colonel, sir, leave this to us!"

"Huh? What are you two doing?" Roy looked around to see the two young sergeants staring at him with determination in their eyes, their hands gripping their weapons tightly.

"We know . . ." Sergeant Natts began. "We know how hard it must have been for you to teach us to do jobs we should already know how to do. We know you're tired . . ."

"We're sorry for making mistakes—we really are, sir! Let us handle this beast! We'll give you three time to escape!"

"What nonsense are you babbling?" Roy shook his head, but Natts and Cayt had already begun walking forward, trembling as they stepped softly through the rocky grass on the hillside, moving themselves between the source of the growling and the officers behind them.

"We're not very good aims, and we don't take orders well. But we can at least buy you some time, sir!"

"Once whatever it is has eaten its fill, I'm sure it will leave you alone! I'm sorry we can't join you on the secret mission, but we go to our deaths proudly, knowing that we saved you, Lord Colonel!"

"You two . . ." Roy was dumbfounded. He hadn't had time to order them back before the low rumbling growl drifted from the bushes again. Roy's ears pricked up. "Huh? Wait a second . . ." He tilted his head into a brisk wind that had blown up, chilling the sweat on his brow; he had noticed something. "Hey," he began, turning to Hughes next to him, "does that sound like . . ."

Hughes had his back to Roy, he was poking one of the two young sergeants on the shoulder. "What if it's still hungry after it eats you, what do we do then?"

"I'm sorry, sir, but I think after then we would have to go in order of ascending rank."

"We'll be waiting for you on the other side, sir!"

"Stop this nonsense and listen to me for just a second, would you? I have a theory," Roy said. His eyes fixed on the two sergeants' grips on their weapons as he spoke, when Armstrong interrupted him with a veritable howl of emotion.

"Never have I seen such devotion!" Tears flowing from his eyes in two waterfalls, Armstrong embraced the two sergeants. "Thinking only of your superior officers! You're amazing!"

"Just hold on, Major," Roy began, but Armstrong could not be stopped.

"Genuine paragons of military men!"

"Major, you're hurting us!"

Armstrong squeezed the two so tightly they could barely breathe. Next to him, Hughes had produced a photo of his beloved daughter from somewhere and began kissing it over and over as he stumbled backward across the rocks toward safety.

"Everybody just calm down and listen to me!" Roy shouted, running ahead to push his way into the thicket from where they had heard the growling.

"Lord Colonel, it's too dangerous!"

"Stay back, sir!"

The two sergeants quailed, certain they were about to see their new superior officer torn limb from limb, but no beast emerged. Instead, a blast of fresh air, cool and crisp—not the thick, wet air of the woods—brushed against their faces.

The thicket ahead of them was dense, but not deep. Beyond,

the view widened. They saw brown rocks, reflecting the sun so brightly that it hurt to look at it after having seen only the dark rock and green of the woods for so long.

"It's not a beast at all. It's just the wind!"

They stood on the edge of a precipice. A crevice opened neatly before them, forming a narrow valley through which the wind blew. This was the source of the low grumbling sound.

The five breathed a communal sigh of relief, then turned their eyes to the edge of the crevice. A single rope bridge swung ahead of them.

"Well, let's get going."

"Onward, onward!"

Suddenly coming back to their senses, Armstrong and Hughes ran forward to cross the bridge.

Roy shook his head. He had already decided he would go no farther, but going back meant descending the sheer cliff they had just climbed. And besides, the view Hughes had been talking about might be right on the other side of this bridge. Shaking his head again, Roy stepped out on the swaying planks.

The first rope twanged at the exact moment that Sergeant Natts stepped on the bridge behind him. Roy froze and slowly turned around. "Wait till we're on the far side, then cross. We don't want to put any more weight on the bridge."

"Right, sir," Natts said, saluting, while Armstrong, Hughes, and Roy shuffled forward, gripping nervously at the swaying rope handles on either side of the bridge.

The wind blew with a loud keen and tussled their hair. When they stopped halfway and looked down, they could see the cliff walls on either side descending to a thin white line, like a thread, at the bottom. It had to be a river, though there was no sound of water. Nor could they judge whether it was an extremely narrow river or an extremely large river from very, very far away. After going a bit farther, the wind against their cheeks became noticeably stronger. At the very middle of the bridge, the wind howled in their ears, and the bridge swayed treacherously.

"You think this bridge is okay?"

"No rocking it on purpose," Armstrong said with a meaningful glare at Hughes.

"Do I look like the kind of guy who would do a thing like that? Of course, if you want me to . . ."

"Rock it, and I shoot you," Roy shouted, the tip of his shoe connecting with a loose piece of wood, knocking it off the edge. The fragment fell spinning out of sight, but they never heard it hit the river below. They watched it fall for some time, then the three looked up at each other.

None of them would admit to being frightened, but their tension carved deep lines in their faces.

Snap.

The sound had been quiet but clear. The three froze.

"You hear that?" Roy asked.

"I might've heard something," Hughes whimpered.

"I heard it, all right," Armstrong said. "I heard it, but I didn't like . . ."

Snap.

Roy looked quickly forward and backward along the bridge. Neither end seemed especially close, but it felt like they were nearer to the opposite side at this point.

"We go forward. Walk slowly," Roy announced to the others, taking a careful step.

The faint snapping sound they heard came almost certainly from the lighter threads in the center of the support ropes. One by one, they broke with a loud, precise "snap!" Even though the wind still howled at their ears, the unsettling sound seemed to reach them with frightening clarity.

Behind them, still on the cliff edge, Natts and Cayt heard it, too.

"Uh-oh . . ." they said in unison, gripping each other by the shoulder, as they watched the three upon the bridge. They wanted more than anything to go help them, but if another person stepped onto those swaying ropes, it would likely send them all to the bottom.

The three already on the bridge stepped forward step by careful step. Each tried desperately not to do anything to hasten the unraveling of their precarious support. For them, each yard seemed like a mile.

Then a high-pitched noise shot through the air, like the whistle of some bird. The entire bridge thrummed like an instrument, the sound shifting from a high pitch to low. Then, there was a moment of silence, followed by a loud snap as one of the bridge's main support ropes gave way.

"I take back my last orders! Run!" Roy shouted, and the three broke into a dash.

The bridge shuddered and began to tilt as the remaining ropes broke one by one. All the boards rattled, the vibrations running through the bridge sending one of the severed ropes snaking up into the air above them, before gravity pulled it down past the bridge toward the depths below.

On the edge of the crevice, Natts and Cayt closed their eyes.

Meanwhile, Roy and the others ran for their lives. With each breaking rope, the bridge rippled like a wave, making it difficult to run upon. They grabbed onto the rope railings so as not to fall, until one of the railings broke free and began to sag.

The bridge gave one final lurch. Roy looked up to see the other side just beyond the swaying hulk of Armstrong in front of him. It seemed close enough that he could reach out and grab it . . .

The last rope connecting the two sides snapped.

For a moment, the three hung floating in the air, as though gravity had decided to wait until they realized what had just happened.

"Aaaaaaugh!"

Their screams echoed through the crevice. When everything fell silent once again, sergeants Natts and Cayt fearfully opened their eyes. Gripping one another by the shoulder, they looked out over the edge. The rope bridge was nowhere to be seen. The wind howled through the rocks below, oblivious to the tragedy that had just taken place.

"Lord Colonel . . ." Natts muttered, dumbfounded. Cayt flopped down on the ground in tears.

"I don't believe it. Colonel, Colonel, Colonel! Colonel?"

The two swooning enlisted men opened their eyes at the same time. There, across the crevice, the wreckage of the bridge hung from a single post, and clinging to that was . . .

"Colonel Mustang!!!"

Armstrong had already made it to the top. He pulled Roy and Hughes up arm over arm as they clung to the remains of the bridge.

"Hooray!" Natts and Cayt shouted as they leapt and twirled in joy.

Meanwhile, on the other side, Roy dropped to his knees and sighed deeply.

"If this is a vacation, I choose work."

Next to him, Hughes and Armstrong echoed his sigh.

"That was a surprise."

"I felt my life shortened by about ten years."

It seemed nothing short of a miracle that they hadn't fallen to their deaths. But the bridge was broken. Roy examined the remains briefly before turning back to Hughes and Armstrong. "We're not getting back this way. We should rest here first and find a place to camp . . ."

"No, let's keep going forward," Hughes stood, cutting off

Roy. "Now that we've come this far, we have to go to the top and walk down the other side anyway, right? No point in standing here! I say let's make some progress while we can. I feel bad about leaving those two sergeants behind, but after everything we've been through, I'm going to see that view."

"That's right, Colonel. We should walk until the sun sets at least. The road from the summit down the other side is gentler, we should be at the bottom by evening tomorrow. Well, unless we encounter some difficult terrain or lose our way . . . Maybe it's safer to say we'll definitely be off this mountain by nightfall two days from now."

Roy was exhausted, both mentally and physically. He wanted nothing more than to lie there on the ground and sleep, but one look at Armstrong and Hughes consulting their maps and picking routes made him realize he didn't have a choice. Roy stood. "How can you even think about tomorrow? I just want to sleep . . ." he grumbled. He turned to shout to Natts and Cayt, still leaping for joy on the far side. "Jump around too much, and you'll fall! We're going down the mountain by a different route. We'll be at the bottom by tomorrow or the next day, or the morning of the third day at the latest . . . so send someone to meet us there! If we aren't there by the fourth day, contact Central. You got that?"

"Yes, sir!"

"Leave it to us!"

The two sergeants waved exuberantly, and Roy looked up at the mountain, wondering if the communications officer would be able to handle such a simple request and dreading the answer. Then, with heavy feet, he began to walk.

THE SUN had already begun to set by the time they neared the summit.

Roy searched the woods in the rapidly fading light for a place where they could camp. He sighed deeply, wondering how a day off could change so quickly into a day of life-threatening adventure, complete with rock climbing and an impromptu bungee jump. He was miserable.

"So where is this view of yours?" he asked, glaring at Hughes. "It's nowhere, that's where!"

Hughes only laughed. "Calm down there, soldier. We'll be walking this mountain all day tomorrow. We'll find it. You should be thinking about getting some rest now that we're finally free of your subordinates, eh? I think it's time for a campfire and some stories."

"How am I supposed to get any rest out here in the middle of nowhere?!" Roy said, his voice a growl through clenched teeth. Suddenly, he saw a red light glimmering through the woods ahead. He squinted his eyes in the gloom, peering through the trees. Now he could see more lights, even the outline of a roof through the trees.

" . . . It's a town."

Hughes and Armstrong looked up.

"A town? Out here? There's nothing on the map."

"I see soft beds and warm food in our future, gentlemen!"

Hughes said with a grin. "See? I was right to keep pushing on."

"Don't act like you're my savior just because we happened to run into a village," Roy said, as dourly as he could manage. But in truth, the mere thought of sleeping under a roof already started to brighten his spirits.

Thanking their fortune, the three began to walk briskly toward the lights.

Closer to the village, the woods looked well maintained. Leaves had been raked into piles for mulch, and branches trimmed here and there to let light through. The closer they got, the more lights they could see beyond the trees, until they could make out at least fifteen structures ahead.

They stepped out of the woods. The village, they could now see, was surrounded on the other side by fields and pasture. They had livestock too, judging by the clucking they could hear in the distance. The road was unpaved, and weeds and flowers grew up between ruts. The delicious smells of dinner cooking and children laughing drifted from the houses alongside the road. A tiny mountain village like any other, except this one wasn't on the map.

They had made it past two houses before someone opened a window and looked out.

"Hey, visitors!" someone shouted. It was a young girl's voice.

Soon, children were looking out of windows and doors throughout the village. Hughes waved a hand in greeting and the children waved back.

"Evening!"

Hughes and Armstrong smiled. "Evening to you, too."

"Look at all the kids," Hughes said. "That's a warm welcome if I've ever seen one."

Within moments, a small crowd of smiling children had gathered by the side of the road, filling the night air with the sounds of talking and laughter. The three stopped, surrounded by children, and waited for the parents to take interest and follow them out. But no adults appeared.

Roy frowned, turning to a girl with long hair who was standing close by. "Excuse me, could one of you call your parents?"

"Our parents aren't here," answered a boy from behind him. The boy was young and had a stern look about him. He stood taller than the other children and might well have been the oldest. Roy guessed his age at around fifteen or sixteen. "They've all gone down to the foot of the mountain to work. If you need something, you can talk to me."

Roy and the others turned, and the circle of children parted to let the boy through toward them.

"How did you get up here?" The boy asked, his piercing blue eyes assessing them from beneath brown locks of hair. A mistrust of strangers was written on his face. Roy swallowed, and as always, Hughes stepped to the occasion.

"We're just passing through is all," he explained. "Came over a rope bridge, but wouldn't you know, it broke, so we were making our way down the mountain when we came across your village."

"You broke the rope bridge?" the boy asked, one eyebrow raised high.

"Sorry, we'll make sure someone comes up to fix it once we're down the mountain."

It wasn't an empty promise. They could call Central as soon as they reached the bottom and requisition men and materials. But Hughes had already decided not to explain himself. For the time being, it was best not to let on that they were military. The children seemed suspicious enough as it was.

"My name is Maes Hughes. This here is Roy Mustang and Alex Louis Armstrong." Hughes put on his friendliest smile and extended a hand. "Tell you the truth, we're bushed from climbing all day, and we're hoping to find a place to stay. There wouldn't happen to be a restaurant or a lodge around here, would there? If not, we're happy to sleep under the eaves . . ."

The boy didn't accept Hughes's hand, instead turning to point outside the village. "Leave," he said coldly.

But the smaller children around him started clapping their hands with enthusiasm.

"We haven't had visitors in such a long time!" one shouted, obviously thrilled.

"How many times do I have to tell you?" the boy said to his charges. "You don't talk to strangers like that. There are bad men out there."

"There you go again, Tild," cut in the girl who had first spoken to Roy. She had a look of utter exasperation on her face.

"Rose . . ." Tild matched her look of exasperation.

"If they were bad men, they wouldn't just come walking in here like this. Why do you always assume the worst?"

Rose seemed to be about the same age as Tild, and from the look on Tild's face, Rose clearly played the role of older sister in the village to Tild's big brother. Tild might be the de facto leader, but the children looked up to Rose, so she shared some of the boy's authority.

"Hughes, Mustang, and . . . Armstrong, was it? My name is Rose. This here is Tild. I apologize on his behalf," she added with a smile.

"Don't worry about it," Roy told her. "I was hoping you hadn't had a string of less than respectable visitors here." He couldn't imagine why anyone would climb all the way up to this village near the summit to do mischief. However, that would explain Tild's lukewarm reception. It would also mean more work for the base. If they couldn't even keep nearby villagers safe, how could they expect public support when something serious happened? Roy glanced over at Hughes and Armstrong, who mirrored his look of concern.

"Not a one. We hardly get any people here at all," Rose explained. "Tild's just overreacting because our parents are away."

"Someone has to take responsibility for this lot," Tild scowled. One of the smaller boys yanked on his hand.

"Hey, Tild. Let's let them stay." The boy's expression made it clear that he was looking forward to having some new people to talk and play with. "Rose has plenty of room, and there's a place to eat."

"That's right, let him stay."

Some of the children grabbed on to Armstrong's massive arms, while others grappled Hughes around the waist in their enthusiasm. None of the children approached Roy with his weary scowl.

Tild's face remained firm. "What if they're robbers? What if they've run out of money and are here to take ours?"

"Well, we're not," Hughes said helpfully.

"We'll pay for our food," Armstrong offered.

Perturbed by Tild's suspicion, the three went for their wallets. At the same time, all three of them stopped, slightly bent over, hands on their empty back pockets.

"Did you all hurt your backs or something?"

Roy frowned. "My wallet's gone."

They all realized simultaneously that their wallets had dropped when the bridge over the crevice had come down. No doubt, their wallets had fallen into the river and washed miles away by now. They groaned. Three grown men without a penny between them. The children fell silent as Tild laughed victoriously.

"See? No money, and a nice story. Pretty suspicious, if you ask me. We don't need you here! And why should we help people who can't pay for their food!"

That would have been it had Rose not spoken up. "So you'd

let them stay if they could pay? How about we have them do something in exchange for money? That would meet your conditions, wouldn't it, Tild?"

"Forget it, Rose. I don't like the look of . . ."

"Tild!" Rose interjected, hands at her waist. "Why must you always be like this? You want all these children to grow up unable to trust a single person they meet?"

Her words hit a soft spot. Tild fell silent.

Rose turned to Roy and the others. "Actually, we did have a lot of rain and wind up here the other day. Some of the roofs need fixing, and our windmill could use some work, too. We don't know when our parents will be back, and we can't have the windmill stopped for so long. Maybe you could help us? In return, we'll give you food and a place to stay. You can do the work tomorrow—let's say a day's work for a night's stay."

"Well, it's a generous offer . . ." Roy said, thinking aloud. He had told the two young sergeants they would be back by morning of the third day, so they had the time. Nor was he adverse to lending a hand, though in all honesty, he had been hoping they would be able to descend the mountain a day early so he could go really enjoy himself somewhere civilized before the men came from the base to pick them up. He felt in need of a vacation now more than ever.

Hughes seemed less conflicted. "Great!" he said enthusiastically, "Then we're all yours tomorrow. I'm ready to work already! I can fix things, and I'm pretty good at paperwork too, if you've got any forms lying around! Oh, and if any of you scamps needs fatherly advice on your love life, why, I'm your man!"

A boy interrupted Hughes's stirring self publicity speech by grabbing his hand. "Come to my house!" The boy said. "We keep all the records on the fields and taxes, but the storm's blown them all over the place. You can help get them back in order!"

"I'm there! Cleaning up messes is my forte."

"How can I help . . ." Armstrong began to speak when his own hand was claimed. A flock of children jumped onto him at once.

"Our roof is leaking!"

"We need to harvest our crop early this year!"

"My desk is broken!"

Armstrong's size got him noticed. One look at his massive frame, and it seemed like half the village was eager to employ him. Within moments, a dozen children hung from his muscled arms.

"I'll do as much as I can, but one job at a time, please." Armstrong grinned, walking around in swift circles despite a classroom's worth of children clinging to him.

Rose caught his eye and pointed toward the windmill in the center of town. "What we really need help on is the windmill, actually."

"Sure thing," Armstrong replied. He had proven to be even more popular than the cheerful Hughes, which left Roy standing all by himself.

Tild stared at the exhausted colonel for a moment, before turning his head and spitting. "So, what can you do? You don't look like you're much good for anything."

Roy had just been wondering if he might get out of this without having to do anything, but the boy's comment irked him. "Hey, I can work, too."

"Yeah? What are your strengths? What do you do normally?"

". . . I analyze situations, make decisions, and give orders. And I do a little teaching as well." Roy said, struggling to explain what he did without admitting he was in the military.

"Teaching? You mean you're a teacher? What do you teach?"

Tild fired question after question at him until Roy ran out of good excuses. He wasn't lying; he did teach. He taught the soldiers at the base down below the mountain. Of course, that hadn't been going well at all. Nor was his work progress exactly stellar back at his regular post at Eastern Command. Roy fell silent, trying to think of something good to say about himself when the girl Rose came to his rescue.

"Maybe you can help at my house, Mr. Mustang. With three guests, there will be plenty of cooking and cleaning to do."

"Can you cook?" Tild asked flatly.

Roy nodded. "I think so."

"*And* clean?"

"If I gave it a shot, sure."

"Laundry?"

"Maybe . . . probably, yeah."

Tild turned to Rose. "Useless."

Roy was too angry and frustrated to reply, but Rose gave a gentle laugh. "It's not all that bad. If there's anything he doesn't understand, I can teach him." She turned back to Roy. "For the time being, you can wash dishes, and wipe the table. I'm sure you'll be able to handle that. So it's decided, then?"

Rose and the other children looked up at Tild. Not even he could deny all those expectant faces.

"Fine. Have it your way."

An exuberant cheer went up from the children then, and the three were, at long last, welcomed into the village.

AFTER SEEING the children back to their homes, Rose led Roy, Hughes, and Armstrong to her house.

Rose's house stood in the middle of the village. It looked larger than most of the houses around it, with walls painted a pleasant cream color. When they walked through the front door, the first thing they saw was a dining hall of sorts, complete with kitchen, counter, tables, and chairs.

"I'm sorry we don't have a proper inn in town," Rose said apologetically. "The first floor here, we keep like this so people can stop by for snacks and tea, but we so rarely have guests for any length of time. I'm afraid there's only one room. Our parents may not be here, but we'll do whatever we can to make your stay pleasant. If you need anything, just let me know."

Rose continued explaining the facilities as she led them

upstairs and opened the door to a large room. In the room were three beds lined up against the wall—the village's only lodgings. Rose began struggling to fix one of the heavy mattresses.

Armstrong landed a hand. "Your parents must be quite busy to leave all of you alone here like this."

"They are," Rose nodded. "Many of our parents are . . . 'technicians,' I suppose you'd call them. They're good with machines and construction. They travel around to far-off towns to help repair damage from the war, so there's always work to be had—too much work. In some families, both of the parents work, and in families where only one parent is skilled, the other follows along to help on the road. Sometimes, they're gone for as long as two months."

"Is that so . . . " Armstrong muttered, wondering how the children managed by themselves for so long.

As Rose said, construction workers and technicians were in short supply and high demand. It was also a time of economic instability, and no matter how much money you had laid away it was no guarantee with market prices for goods fluctuating so rapidly. Stories of parents leaving their children behind to find work weren't uncommon.

Of course, it was the military's job to restore peace and stability so that people didn't have to go to such lengths to enjoy financial security and live with their families. Stories like this reminded him of how much work was yet to be done.

Rose broke the gloomy silence with a laugh. "Sure, we're

lonely, but we're proud that our parents' work helps rebuild the world outside. While they're gone, we look after the fields and the livestock, too. It's more fun than it sounds."

The bed fixed, Rose opened the windows to let in fresh air. She pointed toward the fields across the road below her house. In the dimming dusk, beams of light stabbed out from the windows of the houses that lined the road and illuminated the field. Rose and Roy looked out on fruits and vegetables growing in neatly ordered rows. Even though the lodgings for the night had been unused for some time, they had been kept well cleaned. The children seemed to handle themselves remarkably well in their parents' absence.

"We used to all live farther down the mountain," Rose explained, "but our parents were worried for our safety—there are lots more bandits and the like closer to the road. That's why they made this village here."

"Ah, so the village is new. That's why it wasn't on the map."

"That's right. Unfortunately, that also means some of our relatives and old friends from other towns and villages have stopped visiting us. When our parents aren't here, Tild—he's the oldest—and I are sort of like substitute parents for the other children."

Rose fell silent. The three looked up at her.

"I hope what Tild was saying didn't give you the wrong impression about us. Whenever our parents aren't here, he gets so . . . so harsh. I think he feels like he has to act like an adult, even though he's only fifteen . . . " The uncertainty in her voice made clear the importance she placed on being a good host.

Roy ventured a light smile. "It only makes sense for the eldest to take a stand and size up any potential threats. He's got little children to take care of. I was impressed by how he carried himself, to be honest."

"Really?" Rose gave a sigh of relief, then she put a hand on the door. "I'll call when dinner is ready. You've got lots of work to do tomorrow, so you have to be sure to eat well. Oh, and I'll bring tea up in a bit."

Roy was beginning to understand the social dynamic at work here. Both Tild and Rose had assigned themselves as protectors of the children, but while Tild protected them with strength, Rose protected them with kindness and caring—the same kindness she now directed toward her guests.

Rose walked out. When the door shut behind her, Roy sat down on one of the beds. "So their parents are technicians, huh? Makes sense that they wouldn't be at home, times being what they are."

"With every industry fighting to get back on its feet since the war, technicians are a hot item. Seeing the situation here just makes me think about how much more the military could be doing—should be doing." Hughes slapped a hand down on his knee. "Anyway, we're here for the night. That gives us a whole day to do what we can for these kids as adults, and as soldiers—though I still think it's a good idea we keep mum about who we really are."

"Agreed. It would only make the situation awkward if one of the kids contacted their parents and told them that the military had arrived."

"So now I get to work for my vacation," Roy muttered, wondering how plans for a light hike, fresh air, and an inspiring view could turn to dust so quickly. And that was after a death-defying mountain climb when he was already tired to begin with. Roy grumbled at his own misfortune.

"There, there," Hughes said, comforting him. "Think positively: at least we have beds and food on the way!"

"There's such a thing as thinking too positive!" Roy said with a scowl, but in truth, he had already surrendered to his fate. The way the children had grabbed onto their hands so tightly screamed *please stay with us*. "Fine, We'll work for the day tomorrow. I'll count myself lucky just for the good night's sleep after that climb today. I'm exhausted."

By the time Roy's spirits had picked up again, the door opened, and Rose came in with tea on a platter. "About tomorrow . . . The other children will be here at eight to pick up Mr. Hughes and Mr. Armstrong. Mr. Mustang . . . "

"Please, call me Roy. I'm working for you, after all." Roy took a cup from the platter and flashed a winning smile. Rose smiled back.

"Thank you then, Roy. As I was saying, you have to get up

a little earlier tomorrow. I hope that's all right."

"A little early is no problem. I'll see you in the morning then?"

"Great! I'll come up to get you at five."

Rose closed the door. Leaving Roy to stare at the steam rising from his cup. "Five o' clock . . ." he intoned in a daze.

Next to him, Hughes and Armstrong struggled to hold back peals of laughter.

FIVE O'CLOCK the next morning. Roy opened his eyes beneath warm blankets.

Dawn was approaching. Already, the dim light grew brighter outside the window. Roy cast a sidelong glance at Hughes and Armstrong, still sleeping, and gave a big yawn.

"So sleepy . . ."

He had planned on going to bed right after dinner the night before, but what he hadn't planned on was playing host to practically every kid in the village. While they were eating, kid after kid had come to Rose's door, wanting to meet the visitors. They wanted Roy to tell them stories while he ate, and Hughes and Armstrong found themselves enlisted into giving piggyback rides.

So, while Roy told his bright-eyed audience a yarn about his trip to a faraway town, Hughes made hats and coats out of paper and entertained the children with his usual wit. Next to them, Armstrong had cleared a space of tables and spun in a circle, the children hanging from each arm whooping with laughter as the centrifugal force sent their legs flying up in the air.

When at last they got to bed, Hughes decided to relate a tale of his beloved daughter that lasted a good hour, and unlike Armstrong, who began snoring immediately upon hitting the pillow, Roy learned in excruciating detail all about how to make baby food and the joy of hearing one's child speak her first word. Even after, when the story was done, the wind rattled at the window, and Hughes and Armstrong both snored so loudly that Roy could catch only a few hours of sleep.

He dressed with bleary eyes and went downstairs to find Rose opening windows. A pot of water was already boiling in the kitchen.

"Good morning, Rose."

"Good morning, Roy! Looking forward to your day on the job?"

Rose was not an innkeeper by trade. Today, she would have to feed three adults in addition to her usual chores tending to the fields and livestock. Roy put on the apron Rose handed him without complaint. "So, what do you want me to do?"

"Cleaning, peeling vegetables, and washing the dishes. Afterward, I might have to go fetch some eggs from the coop . . . I'm sorry none of it's very interesting, but we have a lot to do."

None of it did seem very interesting—nor very easy—for

Roy. He began to grow worried. *I'll be fine as long as I don't break any plates,* he told himself, lifting up a chair to get at the floor beneath with his broom.

"Oh, Roy? Be sure to sweep along the floor boards, not against them."

"Y-yeah, right, oops," Roy mumbled sheepishly.

"Oh, and when you're wringing out a towel like that, it's better if you hold your hands facing each other rather than the same way."

"Right, must've forgotten . . ."

Rose gave him helpful advice while she made breakfast. When Roy had finished cleaning up inside, she sent him outside to rake up leaves.

The cold morning air wrapped itself around him. The sun wasn't yet high enough to warm this mountainside village.

"I've completely forgotten how to clean," Roy mumbled to himself. He had never been good at housework, but he *had* done his fair share in the past. However, a few busy years at Eastern Command, and he'd forgotten even the basics. "Maybe I just haven't woken up yet," Roy said. "I sure am sleepy . . ."

A part of Roy had hoped he would be able to take it easy that morning. It was so early that the children were most likely not even up yet. Contrary to his expectations, though, many of the windows in town were already open, and he could hear the sounds of forks on plates and spoons on bowls.

As Roy stood, rubbing his eyes, a young boy ran past. "Morning, Roy!"

"Ah, good morning."

"We've got some vegetables to pick today, so no time to make lunch. We'll be dropping by Rose's for lunch today, okay? See you then!"

"R-Right," Roy stammered, lifting his hand to wave back, but the boy was already gone. ". . . Have fun."

He turned to see another run by. "Morning, Roy! See you at lunch!"

"See you . . ."

"Morning, Roy! Having fun yet?"

One after the other, kids came running out of their houses with baskets and shovels, heading for the fields to the south of town. The sun had only just begun to rise, and already the village was bustling with activity.

A lack of parents seemed to affect the village's daily life far less than Roy had expected.

"Kids sure are amazing . . ." Roy said, stifling a yawn. *And then there's me,* he thought, when a voice from behind interrupted him.

"Ah, so you can sweep."

Tild stood in front of Rosie's house, his eyes filled with the same wary look they'd held when the two first met the night before.

"Good morning," Roy said with as much cheer as he could muster. "Glad to see you approve of the job I'm doing." He gave the ground an extra hard sweep with his brush.

Tild snorted. "I approve of things like fixing the windmill

and organizing our papers, things that we need adults' help with. As far someone who can only sweep . . . But that's not what I came to talk to you about," Tild stared at Roy, a ring of mistrust in his voice.

"What?"

"Tell me why you came here."

"Huh? I said we were just passing through on a hike . . ."

Tild frowned. "It's suspicious. You're suspicious. I don't want mysterious strangers like you in our village."

"Why are we guilty until proven innocent? You sure are a mistrustful kid."

"Always best to err on the side of caution. Anyway, don't even *think* about trying to pull one over on us just because we're children." With that, Tild left. Roy understood Tild was only playing the part of village protector. He admired seeing so much fearlessness in a boy of fifteen. Still, even more than being suspected as a criminal, being called useless twice in two days really got Roy riled up. Roy finished his sweeping in silence.

By the time he went back inside, Rose was making breakfast. "Welcome back. I'm almost done here, if you'd like to eat. When you're not working, you're my guest here, after all."

"I'll eat later," Roy said, eager to make himself useful. "What should I do next?"

"Well, here's a bucket of carrots. Could you go around back and peel these? Here's a knife. Put the peels in this bucket if you would, please." Rose gave him the pile of carrots, the knife, and the bucket, plopped him down in the backyard, and immediately went back into the kitchen to finish up breakfast.

Roy was left holding the knife in one hand, trying to remember how in the world to peel a carrot.

TWO HOURS had passed since the sun rose, when Hughes and Armstrong woke from their restful night, blissfully unaware of Roy's suffering.

After a leisurely breakfast, the first boy came with work, and the two left for their day's chores. Rose sent them off with a smile. "Have fun!" Next to her stood Roy, waving a hand meekly, his fingers wrapped in bandages.

The boy who led Armstrong to the windmill was called Zaj. He had been fond of the big man ever since getting a piggyback ride the night before, and they crossed the fields arm in arm like the best of friends.

"I wish I were as tall as you, Mr. Armstrong. How did you get so big?" the boy asked, looking up at the massively muscled soldier.

"How old are you now, Zaj?"

"Seven. I'm the same age as Luido, but he's bigger than me. It's no fair." The boy frowned and put a hand on his head as if measuring himself against his friend. "I hope to get as big as you someday, Mr. Armstrong."

"I'm sure you will. You know, I was quite the runt when I was a kid."

"Really? Boy, if I were as big as you are, I could fix the windmill all by myself." Smiling, Zaj pointed at a structure ahead of them. The windmill had large, rotating blades made of wood and thick canvas. The night before, when they had seen it standing in the middle of a field from a great distance, it had seemed small and humble, but from this close, it towered over him.

"Cool, huh? My dad built this. It brings water up from beneath the ground. But the rainstorm the other day damaged the blades, and they aren't spinning as well as they used to. We were worrying what we'd do if we had to wait until our parents got back."

The windmill itself was built of stone, and a small door had been cut at its base. Armstrong hunched down to peer inside. "Amazing!"

Even to an amateur's eyes, the windmill was impressively built. At its top it must have stood thirty feet high. A small staircase wound up along the inside, giving access to the windmill mechanism. Inside, rings of iron reinforced the structure. The outer wall was made of carefully stacked bricks. Several ropes hung straight down from the main axle, disappearing into a large hole in the floor. With every turn of the wheel, one of the ropes would lift, carrying a bucket of water up from some underground reservoir.

"Where does the water go?"

"Over here."

Armstrong stepped back outside, and Zaj pointed to the

side of the windmill tower. A hole had been cut in the side, out of which ran a small channel filled with water.

"The buckets of water catch on the edge of the channel here and spill water into it. The channel runs all the way down to the fields."

Armstrong looked down the simple aqueduct until it disappeared into the rich green of the village fields. Normally, water was a real problem in higher elevations where rivers didn't run, but instead of finding a place closer to water, Zaj's father and the other villagers had built this carefully planned windmill out of iron and stone to bring the water to them. Not only did it bring the water to them, but it saved them hours and hours of labor by delivering it precisely to where it was needed most: the fields.

Armstrong was deeply impressed. It took no small amount of technical skill to craft a windmill this large, and Zaj's father must have taken great care in designing it to make it so easy to use.

"This is a fine piece of work here," he commented. "Your father must be quite skilled."

Zaj grinned and looked embarrassed. He scratched his head. "My dad was an engineer for a steelworks. He was always making bridges and that sort of thing. I'm studying to become an engineer just like him. See, I made that."

Zaj pointed a short distance down the aqueduct to where a tiny toy bridge stood over a thin stream of water—the overflow from the channel.

"I see!" Armstrong said, walking over. He noticed that he

had built not only a small bridge but a miniature watermill to go with it. Either would fit in the palm of his hand, but despite their size, both were sturdily built from tiny chiseled stones and strips of iron. Each looked every bit as impressive as the larger versions behind him, considering that they had been built by a boy of seven. Clearly, Zaj took great pride in his father's work.

"You've got a bright future ahead of you if you can make things like this, Zaj."

"Really? You think so? Once I'm big enough to fix the real thing, I hope I can work with my dad and the others."

"That's right," Armstrong said, smiling gently at the grinning boy. "But stay out of the real windmill until you're bigger. It's too dangerous. Wait here while I check on those blades."

"Right!"

Armstrong patted the boy on the head and went back inside the windmill. He climbed the staircase carefully, as it lacked any railings. When he reached the break lever for the windmill mechanism, he gave it a yank, and the giant blades slowly ground to a halt. From there, he needed only to push up a hinged panel in the ceiling to gain access to the roof, where he could check each blade for damage and look down at the central axis.

Armstrong busily scraped a wattle of leaves off one of the blades with his hands as a gentle breeze began to blow. From his vantage point on the top of the windmill, he could see the entire village. There was Roy, wiping windows at Rose's house, and the local children on their way back from the fields, playing by the roadside. And there was Hughes, running along with them.

He thought how odd it was, seeing his two companions and himself out of uniform. Back on base, they walked briskly through the halls, barking orders, doing paperwork. Yet one night in the village, and already they were on its clock. Time moved slower here, and Armstrong found he rather enjoyed the change.

Armstrong's solid sense of justice made him the perfect fit for the military, but he disliked people brandishing their authority and abhorred harming others for no reason other than to follow orders. The importance of duty paled in comparison with the village's slower, easier pace and the opportunity to help he found there.

He looked across the village, spotting boys working in the fields and girls feeding the livestock. Near the front of the windmill, Zaj played with his toy bridge. It occurred to Armstrong that Zaj didn't just want to become an engineer out of pride for his father's work; he wanted to pursue the profession out of a desire to be with his parents more.

The children in this village were mature beyond their years, but their loneliness seemed apparent from the attention he and the others had received the night before. Armstrong carefully continued his inspection of the windmill blades.

He knew he would leave the next day, but he resolved to spend as much time as he could with the children until then.

HUGHES HAD FINISHED with a brief tutoring assignment and was on his way to Luido's house. Luido had asked him the day before to help sort scattered documents. He knew just where Luido's house was, but when he got there, he found he had arrived too early. He decided to spend some time walking around looking at the other nearby houses. When they had arrived the night before, it had been too dark to see the town clearly. Under the bright sun, he noticed that each house had a unique design from the others.

"Quite the craftsmanship," Hughes said, standing in front of one particularly colorful house. A wooden swing rocked on the front porch, and a slide made out of metal extended from the second floor. He had only ever seen a slide in someone's garden, never one leaving from the house itself. It was an interesting idea.

He saw individual touches on other houses: one had a fireman's pole, another was designed so that the whole house looked like some kind of animal.

"It's like a big amusement park," Hughes said to himself, when a thought occurred to him. "Why, I should make a swing for Alicia!" He smiled, imagining his daughter playing on a swing of her very own.

Thus he went around looking at the houses, filing away ideas for other things he might make until he had come clear to the edge of the village.

Suddenly, a figure appeared in the woods ahead. It was Tild. He emerged from an overgrown thicket and wiped dirt off his white shirt and arms. He walked toward a small pump at the edge of the wood. Grass grew up around its base, making it look half abandoned. Without so much as a glance in Hughes's direction, he began to draw water from the pump.

"Hello there, Tild!" Hughes called out.

The boy turned, his face tense for a moment. He could hear the growl in the boy's throat even from this distance. "Aren't you going to Luido's house? It's the other way," Tild said coldly, but Hughes's enthusiasm was not so easily diminished.

"Oh, I know that. I had a little time, so I was just checking out the village."

"'Checking out'?" Tild asked, his eyes narrowed in suspicion.

Hughes laughed and waved a hand. "Don't make those faces. I was just impressed at all of the different houses you have up here. You don't see this kind of creative design much in the towns below." He glanced at the window of a nearby house. Various animal shapes had been carved into the wooden frame. "I heard from Rose that your parents built all these? I caught a glimpse of your place back there. Those window frames are really impressive. And the iron struts on the roof, they kind of made it look like a sailing ship. It's pretty cool."

"Zaj's dad made those. The window frames were Rose's father. My dad designed the house, though. It was supposed to look like a boat."

"Neat, a 'boat'-house."

Tild couldn't help but blush. It was the first time Hughes had seen anything approaching happiness on the boy's face.

Though the corners of his eyes and the cut of his jaw made him look old behind his years, when he smiled, the boy in him shone through.

"I've got a daughter, you know. Seeing all these houses has got me to thinking I should make something for her. Say, you think any of these other houses might have any good ideas? Oh, hey, would you like to see her picture? I'll show it to you, as long as you promise not to fall hopelessly in love!"

Hughes took the photograph out of his shirt pocket and grinned, but Tild just shook his head. "No, thanks." Head still turned, he pointed back toward the village. "If you want ideas for toys, check out the house over there."

The house he was pointing at had a little red roof and a porch swing. Several animals carved of wood frolicked on the front lawn. It was just the kind of thing to excite a little girl. *Maybe I've softened him up a little,* Hughes thought. *Sure took long enough.* To Tild he said, "Looks great, thanks!"

"Don't mention it."

Even in kindness, Tild's voice held little warmth. Hughes grinned, but Tild noticed and answered him with a scowl. "What are you looking at?"

"I was just thinking that maybe you're not such a stick in the mud after all."

"Leave me alone!" Tild said, raising a hand, but just then they heard a boy's voice calling from back in the village.

"Mr. Hughes! Where are you?"

Hughes glanced down at his wristwatch. It was time for him to start his next job.

"Stop wasting time with me. You've got work to do!" Tild said gruffly.

"Right!" Hughes replied with a wry smile at the still blushing boy. He turned and ran back into the village. Before long, he spotted Luido waving his hand from the window of a brick house.

"Sorry to keep you waiting. Say, you've got a nice place too, Luido."

Indeed, the craftsmanship in this house's construction put to shame everything he had seen in town. It was a small house, but tall, with five stories. Geometrical patterns adorned the railings that ran up the stairs. A wooden horse rocked on the front door patio.

"I just told my dad what kind of house I wanted, he designed it, and everybody in town helped build it. There's lots of stuff inside. Come on in!"

True enough, the inside of the house didn't disappoint. Hughes saw handmade furniture and toys. There was a desk made of curved boards, without a straight edge on it. A model train made of delicately welded plates ran along the floor, and a child's car with large metal wheels sat parked against a wall. The night sky, complete with constellations, had been painted on the ceiling. Everything looked as though it had jumped out of some children's book.

Hughes ran his hand over what looked like a handmade camera and looked up at the bookshelves that had been built along one wall. The shelves were stuffed with picture books.

"Let me guess. You like stories, Luido?"

"I love them!"

"I had a feeling."

Hughes had seen enough houses in town to begin to understand what was going on. He would rather spend time with his daughter than give her things, but that wasn't an option the parents here had. So they used their considerable skills to pour their love and affection into houses and toys. Luido's house came straight out of a fairy tale. The walls of the house where he had tutored a girl had been covered with carvings of her favorite animals. The houses in this village had been designed to put smiles on children's faces even when their parents were away.

As a parent, Hughes understood how they felt all too well.

Luido walked down a hallway, passing by storybook scenes painted on the walls, and led Hughes to a room at the back of the house.

"This is what I wanted your help with," Luido said. He picked up one of the many papers that lay scattered about the room and handed it to Hughes. "One of the windows broke in the storm, and all these papers got blown about. I don't understand what they say, so I wasn't able to put them in any kind of order."

Bookshelves on each wall reached to the ceiling, stuffed with stacks of documents. Haphazardly piles of papers were scattered across the desk and even on the floor.

Hughes looked at the paper in his hand, then pulled a few random papers off the shelves and read them, too. Some listed field acreage and owner names. Others recorded taxes paid, and still others even documented complete family records for the village.

"Your house keeps all the records for the town?"

"Mom did most of it, but she left to help dad at work. I was supposed to keep watch over these while they were gone . . . now I don't know what to do."

"Don't worry," Hughes said, putting his hand on the boy's shoulder. "Leave your documents to me. I'll even teach you how to mark them so they are easier to sort in the future. That way, you'll be able to do it yourself. Want to try?"

Luido's face suddenly brightened. "Yes! Yes please!"

Luido rushed to find paper and a pen, and when Hughes began explaining his system, the boy listened intently. The look on his face as he listened and the way he gripped his pen reminded Hughes of his daughter as she drew pictures or listened with rapt attention as he told a story.

"Right, first you want to draw a straight line at the top . . ." As he patiently explained his system to Luido, he found himself thinking of his daughter waiting for him back home. He wanted to rush home and build her a swing, so that she might be happy on days when his work kept him from being with her. Hughes smiled inside thinking of the look she would have on her face when he came home, swing set in tow.

WHILE HUGHES and Armstrong had been enjoying the slower pace of village life, Roy found himself engaged in solo battle with a mountain of vegetables.

Rose was baking cookies in the kitchen, leaving Roy alone in the back garden. He sat there in the warm sunlight, knife in hand, listening to the sound of himself peeling carrots. His arm had begun to ache from the repetitive motion. He felt like his back would be forever frozen in a permanent hunch. When he stood up to stretch, his spine made disturbing popping noises.

"This is brutal," he muttered, walking around to the front of the house to look out over the fields across the road. Time had passed rapidly while he had been running around trying to help, and now the sky above his head had turned a rosy red color.

The sound of laughter caught his ear, and he glanced down the road to see Armstrong helping children pile freshly picked vegetables into baskets. He would pick up a basket, often with a kid or two attached, and carry them across the fields back to the road. Now and then, he would stop to mend a broken fence or otherwise help wherever the children asked for it.

In a small clearing next to one of the fields, Roy spotted Hughes sitting with an open book, reading to some children. Other children gathered nearby, and though they weren't listening to the story, they seemed to enjoy just being around him, jumping rope, and playing catch.

It was enough to bring a smile to Roy's lips, and it made his dreary work in the army seem like a distant dream. But this was reality, as the cuts on his hands from chopping carrots proved.

Roy slowly walked around to the back garden, his shoulders rising and falling with a long sigh.

I washed dishes, I swept, I peeled.

None of these were things he did regularly. He had done all of them in survival training long ago, but when it came to actually putting them into practice, he was hopeless. A pile of thick peels lay at his feet, and the basket next to him brimmed with vegetables, all of which had ended up much smaller than when he began. In another basket by his feet waited the rather large mountain of vegetables he had yet to attack.

"Useless," he muttered, remembering what Tild had said the night before. Roy had been doing military work so long, he figured he could do anything when put to it. He had forgotten just how hard housework could be. Here he sat, despondent, unable to perform the simplest of tasks.

Rose remained kind and considerate throughout the day. Whenever she came to see how he was doing and offer advice, he felt even worse, like he was holding her back from her own chores.

It's too bad they don't need any emergency training here, or anyone to show them how to use their weapons.

"What they need—what *I* need—is peeler training."

From far off came the sounds of children playing, mingled with Hughes and Armstrong's laughter. Roy sat alone, staring at his vegetables until Rose called out to him. "Something on that carrot?" She came out the back door and handed him a freshly baked cookie. "Taste this for me, would you? You don't look so well. Are you okay?"

"No, just astonished at my own ineptitude," he said grimly, taking a bite of the cookie. "No matter how many times I ask the same questions I still keep making the same mistakes . . . Can't say I've been much of a help."

"Of course you've been a help. I couldn't have gotten half the things done that I did this morning without you. And you cut firewood—I've never been any good at that."

"Maybe I did that one thing well, but everything else has been a disaster. Sorry."

Rose shook her head. "Not at all. How about the eggs?"

"Eggs?"

"You didn't break a single one of those eggs you brought me."

Dimly, Roy recalled visiting the chicken coop after lunch. True, he hadn't broken a single egg, but only because the chickens had been miraculously calm and cooperative.

"Those chickens get all excited whenever I go in there. They break eggs right and left. Sometimes they chase after me. That's why I sent you in."

"Heh, is that so?" Roy asked, his mood feeling lighter

already. To be sure, collecting eggs was no great feat, but it felt good to have done at least something right that day, and he told Rose as much.

She smiled and picked up one of the carrots he had peeled. "I expect every kid in town will be here for dinner tonight. Let's get cooking!"

"I'll be the waiter. I can do that at least."

"I sure hope you can! Let's do our best."

Our best, she said. She means we're a team, Roy thought. The sentiment meant everything to him.

AS ROSE HAD predicted, by nightfall, the first floor dining hall was filled with children. Many of them had come to say good-bye to their visitors. After spending all day helping the children, Armstrong and Hughes had become quite popular, and everyone wanted to sit by them, talking and joking with them while they ate.

They even chatted with Roy, who busily waited tables. He tried to keep up with the conversations as he weaved his way around chairs, trays of dishes balanced precariously in his hands.

"Soup over here, please!"

"I want one of those tomato salads!"

"Hold on a second. Right, so that's soup, tomato salad, soup . . ." Roy repeated the orders to himself as he rushed between the tables to the kitchen. Once the bowls had been delivered, he picked up a tray of empties, brought them back to the sink, and began washing dishes until Rose called out to him.

"Aren't you tired, Roy? You can go out and eat if you want—it's all right."

"No, I'll work a bit more. I said I'd be the waiter, and I mean to do it," Roy declared as he gave the cup he was holding a final wipe. He felt he owed it to Rose. She had helped him tirelessly, teaching him how to peel vegetables, and never once complained, even when he broke one of her dishes. Of course, he risked breaking more dishes if he kept washing, but even so he couldn't sit down.

"Only if you're sure. Here, can you bring this to Hughes?"

"Got it."

Tray balanced carefully in his hand, Roy walked over to the table where Hughes was sitting. Hughes looked up with a grin and grabbed Roy by the apron. "You look good in that."

It was a simple chef's apron made of light brown cloth, thankfully not some frilly lacy thing. Roy set the dish down on the table and squatted until his eyes were on a level with Hughes.

"If you so much as whisper about this to anyone at Eastern Command . . . You know what I'm saying, right?"

Roy's subordinates at Eastern Command loved nothing more than to pick on their superior officer, and Hughes had always been their go-to man for embarrassing moments and painful memories. If word about this got out, he would never hear the end of it. The upper crust of Eastern Command, the feared and respected fire alchemist Roy Mustang, wearing an apron and waiting tables.

"At ease, soldier. Your secret is safe with me," Hughes whispered back with a smile. He turned to his food.

"How is it?" Roy asked. Truth be told, he was more nervous about the food than about how he looked in an apron.

"Not bad. Wait, you didn't help cook this, did you?"

Hughes's eyes widened. "I'm impressed!"

"I was in there with my knife, chopping away all day," Roy said with a self-satisfied chuckle. "See those greens on the side there? I cut those. I cut 'em good."

Hughes looked at the ragged sprig of parsley clinging for dear life to the edge of his plate. He sank toward the table, shaking his head, while Roy stood grinning. Next to them, Luido, Zaj, and several other boys and girls were clinging to Armstrong's arms and legs.

"Spin us around like you did yesterday!"

"I'll do better than that!" Armstrong shouted. Standing up he ripped off his shirt and tossed it to the floor.

"Woooh!"

Armstrong roared with laughter. His peers in the military knew his ripping-off-the-shirt shtick well, but for the kids, it was a show like none other. The crowd clapped and cheered.

"Armstrong! Armstrong! Spin us around!"

"Me too!"

"Don't tire him out, now," Rose cautioned the children softly as she sat a tray of desserts on the table. "Thanks for playing with all the children like this, Mr. Armstrong."

"Not at all. I'm the one who should be thanking you. I've never seen such a friendly bunch of kids. You're like one big, happy family."

"That's what I like about our town. Everybody helps each other out—like we really are all brothers and sisters. You know, when the grown-ups are here, they're the same way, playing with all of us, whether we're actually their children or not."

"Well, sounds like we've got a reputation to live up to, then," Armstrong said. "Care for a spin, Miss Rose?"

"Oh, but I'm bigger than the other children . . . and heavier," Rose said, though the tug-of-war between eagerness and responsibility stood out clearly on her face.

Armstrong winked. "It's perfectly safe. I've got faith in my muscles." He tensed a bicep, and the muscles rippled along his arm. Rose's eyes went wide, and she giggled.

"All right!"

Rose jumped and Armstrong plucked her lightly out of the air. "Here goes!"

Across the table, Hughes was lifting the smaller children high above his head. Rose's house was filled with even more laughter and merriment than the night before.

While the children and Rose laughed and had fun, Roy picked up a candle and a light bulb and walked outside to check on the front porch lamp. It had been flickering earlier and was probably due for a change.

For all the merriment inside, Roy looked at the children and saw sadness lingering at the corners of their eyes. With only this one last night left with their guests, they had clearly decided to make the most out of the evening. It fell to them to give the kids what they wanted, and Hughes and Armstrong were more than up to the task. *Once I'm done with the dishes, maybe I'll join them,* Roy thought. He reached out for the lamp on the unlit porch, when he heard voices drifting toward him from the darkness of the road.

"Hey, Tild! I just got a ride from Mr. Armstrong!"

"Huh, no kidding."

It sounded like Tild and Zaj. Zaj's voice sang with exuberance, but the older boy sounded as grumpy as ever.

"We've never had fun guests like these! I wish Mr. Armstrong and Mr. Hughes would stay longer! Why don't we ask them?"

Light from the other houses showed the village in vague, amorphous shadows, yet Roy could see Tild and Zaj nowhere. Still, he could tell from the tone of Zaj's voice how much he had grown fond of their visitors. Tild's voice, by contrast, remained cold.

"We can't let them. They can't stay."

"Why not?"

"The grown-ups who come to our village don't come here to live, Zaj. They're just passing through."

"I know, but . . ."

"Let it go."

"But . . . but it's so lonely here! You're always shut up in your house, and you never play with us . . . I went there and knocked today, and you didn't even answer the door!"

"I told you not to come to my house during the day. I have to focus on my work. How many times do I have to tell you?"

Roy felt the shift in the boy's tone, and fearing that saying something would only earn him another menacing glare, he focused on fixing the lamp. The light flickered on, revealing the arguing boys a little way down the road.

Tild's shirt and arms were caked with mud from the fields. When the light flickered on, Tild noticed they had company and turned his back, the anger plain on his face. Zaj merely stood there on the verge of tears. He hadn't seen Roy.

"I don't like you anymore, Tild. Mr. Armstrong and them are much nicer! I hate you!" Zaj's words, so simple and so clear, cut like a knife. Large tears running down his cheeks, the younger boy ran past Roy into Rose's house.

Tild stood alone in the glow of the front porch lamp. A single tear ran down his cheek. "I told you I didn't want you here," he said, glaring at Roy. "Grown-ups come visit us, but they always have to leave. They're nice enough when they're here, but they don't care enough to stay." Tild's voice rose from a hush to a shout. "It's not fair! I have to work all day! I have to give up everything for them . . . and they hate me! You just come in here, and because you're adults, they instantly trust you! I can't do this anymore!"

"Tild," Roy called out.

The boy's face twisted in pain. He whirled away. "You can stay here and watch the children. I'm through with it!"

Tild began to run and soon vanished in the night.

Rose stepped out onto the front porch. "Where's Tild, Roy? Zaj was crying."

"They were fighting about something . . . Do Tild and the other children not get along?" Since their welcome to the village, Roy had assumed Tild was the leader of the children. He imagined him as a surrogate parent, in a way, but there was clearly a rift between him and Zaj. Come to think of it, Tild hadn't showed his face last night or tonight at Rose's house when they played with the children. He had chalked it up to the boy's distrust of the guests, but maybe Tild just didn't care to spend time with the other children.

Rose looked out at the empty street, a frown on her face. "Ever since we moved the village, Tild stays inside most of the time. He gave up studying ship design and just works on repair jobs he gets from down the mountain. He doesn't play with the other children, and the way he talks . . . Well, it's not hard to see why lots of the kids avoid him." Rose sighed. "I'm sorry you had to see this on your last night. Don't worry about Tild. Let's go back inside. The other kids want to play with you too, Roy."

"I've got all I can handle just waiting tables," Roy said gently.

Rose was much more worried than she let on. He followed her back inside, taking one glance back over his shoulder in the direction Tild had run. He could see nothing but the road stretching into darkness.

BY THE TIME the three soldiers had seen the children home and returned to their rooms, the night had grown late. They quickly reviewed their next day's route to the bottom and went straight to bed.

"All in all, I had a great time," Hughes said, hugging his pillow. He rolled over and looked up at the ceiling. "I enjoyed playing with the kids, and I even learned how to make a swing set."

"I could get used to doing this every once in a while," Armstrong agreed. "And I just might. They were practically begging for us to come back, after all."

As Hughes and Armstrong smiled, whispering about how much they had enjoyed their unexpected side trip, Roy lay with his chain on his pillow, frowning.

"What's wrong, Roy?"

"Nah, I'm just thinking about Tild."

When the boy had left the night before, he seemed ready to wash his hands of the village and all the children living there. He had even suggested in an offhand way that Roy and the others should take care of the children, but Roy felt pretty sure that didn't mean the boy trusted them. Though he might not suspect them of being burglars, like he did when they first arrived, his attitude had changed little, even after they spent the whole day helping out. Perhaps one day wasn't long enough for his demeanor to soften, but Roy still couldn't see why everything the boy said seemed sharp-edged.

"I think Tild picked me out as his favorite person to hate, but even still, what's with that kid's attitude?"

Hughes rolled over so he was facing Roy. "He's mad, is all."

"Mad? At what?"

"Well . . ." Hughes told them about his meeting with Tild by the woods earlier that day. "He almost warmed up to me when I complimented him, but when I pointed that fact out to him, he went back to his old, sour self. He's got issues with adults, that much is certain. Haven't a clue what they might be, though."

"I figured it was something like that."

Roy knew he was no judge of the children's soul, but he sat there thinking for a while, wondering how he could possibly understand this boy with whom he had barely been able to communicate. "Not that I'm a stranger to being disliked," Roy mumbled. He sat up in bed and reached for the lamp.

Tomorrow they would go down the mountain. They would probably never see Tild again, and that would suit the boy just fine. Perhaps the kindest thing to do would be to leave him alone. The only thing remaining for Roy now was to get some sleep.

"We're leaving tomorrow morning at nine, so nobody sleep in," Roy said, blowing out the lamp and lying down with a sigh. "I'm bushed. I tell you, housework is hard."

The moment Roy's head hit the pillow, Hughes began to regale him with a tale of his daughter. "Speaking of housework, my Elicia . . ."

Knowing the long, convoluted tale that was about to begin, Roy held up his hand for silence. "No stories, please."

Hughes pushed his hand down. "No, no, listen! See when I get up in the morning . . ."

"I don't care. I'm going to sleep. You sleep, too." Roy pulled his comforter up over his head.

"No really, she's so sweet. She brings up a plate in her little hands . . ."

Armstrong rolled over to face the wall. "I'll be catching some sleep, too. Goodnight."

"Then consider the story a lullaby. See, my daughter . . ."

"Sleep!"

Hughes knocked aside the pillow thrown at his head and took cover under his own blankets. He kept talking, occasionally chuckling at his own story, while outside the wind howled in the forest.

WHEN THEY WENT downstairs the next day, the first floor was filled with kids who'd come to send them off. Roy, Hughes, and Armstrong went around, patting the children on the head, saying their farewells. Tild was nowhere to be seen, either inside the house or in the fields.

Roy didn't like to leave on bad terms, but he had decided

not to worry about the boy anymore. Whatever his problems were, as visitors, Roy, Hughes, and Armstrong had no right to interfere. If they stayed longer in the village, he would only grow to hate them more, and Roy had places to go, regardless.

Still, one thing bugged Roy. He could take the cold shoulder, but being called "useless" cut too deep. Roy told Hughes and Armstrong to wait a while, and he walked off toward the livestock hut. During his work the day before, the one thing he'd done well had been collecting eggs from the coop. He had time for one last trip, a last-ditch effort to clear his name and show his gratitude to Rose for all her patience.

The hens didn't stir when Roy walked in and gave no resistance when he took the eggs. "Good girls, there. And no pecking at Rose, you hear?" Satisfied, Roy left the coop.

With the still-warm eggs in his hands, Roy looked up at the cloudless sky.

Down at the base, his training duties awaited his return. The men would come to him, all nervous, asking him to teach them how to do everything. Yet for some reason, the thought of answering their questions didn't make him irritable anymore. He had been mad—furious, even—at his subordinates for coming to him with questions about the most basic things, but now it occurred to him that these tasks he considered simple weren't easy for them at all.

Roy chuckled to himself. "Maybe I learned something."

He had assumed the men came to him for directions because they were afraid of failing and being yelled at. But now he realized they simply didn't want to be a burden. Just like when he had asked Rose where to put the plates or how to scrub a pot.

And Rose had never been mad, had never sighed. He remembered when she offered to take him under her wing, saying "if there's anything you don't understand, I'll teach you." And she had, many times.

Roy closed his eyes, smiling as a cool breeze blew against his face. *Maybe I'll be a better teacher now back at the base.*

Roy began walking back toward Rose's house and the others, when something caught his eye. Something small and metallic in the woods reflected the light of the sun. He stepped into the undergrowth and caught the morning sun rising over the mountains ahead of him. Roy held up his hand against the bright glare when he saw a large boulder sitting deeper in the woods. The metallic object lay at its foot.

Roy walked through the trees, the only sound being the low moan of the wind. He quickly found the piece of metal and picked it up. It was caked with mud. He scratched at it with his finger, his eyes going wide. "What's this doing here?"

It was a shell casing.

Roy found it hard to believe that any of the children left alone in this village were allowed to use a rifle. *Wasn't Hughes saying last night that he had run into Tild in this part of the woods yesterday?* Roy rubbed his chin.

In fact, something had bothered him when he heard Hughes's story the night before. Even though Zaj had been mad at Tild for "staying inside all day and not answering his door," Hughes had run into the boy outside, in the middle of the day. The two stories didn't add up. Roy had chalked it up to bad timing. Even if the boy did work at home, he would certainly go outside sometime. But now that he had found a shell casing in the woods where Tild had been seen the day before, he started to wonder.

Roy put down his eggs and recalled the argument Tild and Zaj had the night before out in front of Rose's house. One of his hands strayed to his shirt front. Tild's shirt had been muddy there. His arms had been muddy too, from the wrists to the elbows. Roy tried to think of a position that would muddy only one's forearms when it came to him.

Roy looked up at the boulder. It stood a little taller than he did, but it had plenty of handholds. He quickly climbed up. The top of the boulder was flat—just wide enough for a man to lie down—and it was covered in dry leaves and grass. Roy knelt down and looked out through the woods, away from the village. From here he had a clear view of the main path leading down the mountainside. Marks in the leaves suggested that someone had been lying here, and when Roy mimicked that position, he got dirt on his shirt and both his arms.

It was easy to picture Tild lying here, a rifle cradled in his arms. So he had lied, saying he was in his house doing repair work, when he was out here with a gun. From atop this boulder, Tild could sit on lookout and occasionally fire warning shots to make sure strangers didn't approach the village if he didn't like how they looked. Rose had said they received few visitors because their village had just relocated, but no doubt Tild's guard duty helped further reduce that number.

Why would he go to such lengths to keep outsiders away? What made him so suspicious?

The wind blew through Roy's hair as he sat contemplating this. The gentle blowing of the wind made a low murmur that moved through the woods. Roy turned. The sound was surprisingly like the one they had heard the other day by the rope bridge.

"What's that?"

He had been hearing the wind since they arrived in the village, but he had merely chalked it up to strong winds this high up the mountain. Now, as he listened more closely, it sounded like the specific sort of sound of wind blowing through a deep crevice or valley—a low howling, like a beast, here in this wood. Roy walked a distance through the trees, pushing aside the underbrush until he came to a small, rock-filled gully. He heard the sound again, closer this time. Roy pricked up his ears, trying to determine the source. Eventually, he found a gap between two boulders wide enough for a person to pass through.

The wind shooting through the gap was the source of the howl. On closer inspection, Roy found that the placement of rocks seemed unnatural, compared to the landscape around them. In fact, he grew ever more certain that this was man-made. From the sound of the wind, the space on the other side of this gap must have been rather large. He put his hand on the edge of the rock, about to go in, and something black and sticky stuck to his fingers. Roy held his hand up to his face and smelled oil.

Roy forced his way through, heedless of the oil staining his clothes.

It was pitch black inside. Roy stumbled and kicked something with his foot. It made a metallic rattling that echoed through the space inside. From the sound, Roy guessed he was in a very large cavern. Roy reached down and found that the object he had kicked was a lamp. He picked it up.

After smelling the air carefully for gas, Roy pulled a single glove from his pocket and put in on his hand. The glove had an alchemical circle drawn on it.

Even before he made a gesture with his hands, touching his finger to the circle and creating a lick of flame to light the lamp, Roy had an idea of what he would see.

There in the large cavern several steel frames had been strewn about. He saw two hoops, like wheels, and rods with gears on them, lying between sheets of curved metal. At a glance, it seemed like so much junk, but to a military man like Roy, it was ominous. Though it seemed a lot of parts were still missing, he knew what one could make if you put all the parts lying there together.

A few thoughts struck Roy in rapid succession. They all had to do with Hughes and Armstrong's aborted mission to find the hidden weapons stash.

The village they had gone to had turned out to be abandoned.

And here they were, in a brand-new village.

A village filled with skilled engineers and craftsmen.

And the boy, Tild, so afraid of outsiders—was protecting something.

"Looks like I've found those weapons. Or should I say, weapon." Roy whistled quietly. The parts filling the cavern, when put together, would form a cannon bigger than a railway car.

TILD CAST a disparaging look at the man standing in front of his door. He didn't even try to drive him off.

"You knew, didn't you?"

Roy stepped inside Tild's house. His clothes were filthy with stains from the old oil that coated the walls of the cannon's hiding place. The oil had sunk into the rock, turning black and giving off a peculiar scent. Tild noticed the stains but said nothing.

"That's why you were so suspicious of us. No, not just us. You didn't want any visitors to your little village, did you?"

Tild had been driving people off since the village moved, Roy figured. It all made sense. When they had arrived in the village, Tild had showed up later than the other children, and when they told him how they had got there, by the rope bridge, he had frowned. He had been watching only the main path up to the village.

"Well?" Tild said, his eyes moving to look at Roy. "So now

you know everything. What will you do? Are you going to tell the military? Or maybe sell the information to someone else?" Tild spoke carelessly, as though he didn't really care what happened in the end. "Do whatever you like."

He had said these same words to Rose and the other children when they decided to let Roy and the others stay.

"It doesn't matter how hard I try, it all comes to nothing in the end."

Roy could hear the fatigue of long months spent holding a dark secret in the boy's voice.

"None of the other kids know?"

Tild snorted and smiled a bored sort of smile. "Of course not. I'm not about to tell them their parents make weapons that kill people. They all think our parents are out there helping rebuild the country."

Factories competed fiercely for military arms contracts. Roy knew the factories aggressively courted people with skill, hoping to get an edge over their rivals. Construction, shipbuilding, and even munitions manufacture all required metal. That made anyone who knew how to work with metal valuable. And someone who might potentially improve the technology available to a munitions factory would be prized highly indeed.

It made sense that the parents of the children who lived in this town would be top on many factories' wanted lists. They might have started out in more innocent careers, but offers too good to turn down would have come sooner or later. They probably didn't have the heart to tell their children they weren't building houses and fishing boats anymore. Only Tild, the eldest, knew the truth.

"As if the military really cares what happens to us," Tild said, spitting out the words with a sudden anger. "They gather up all these technicians and say it's for the good of the country, but they don't care about us. They just want to win their stupid wars and boast about their accomplishments. And they keep all the good equipment to themselves, because they have all the money. Our parents have trouble just holding on to their jobs. And now, because they're working on weapons, even our homes are military targets . . . it's ridiculous."

The military had never ordered a factory to hire technicians, but that was hardly a defense, and Roy knew it. It was common practice to go to already overworked factories, the ones with the best technology, and to give them orders for weapons. It worked a bit like Roy's subordinates at Eastern Command coming to him for his opinions on proposals the day he had to leave. If you go to somebody who already has too much on his plate and ask him to do more, either he refuses you, as Roy had, or he goes looking for more hands. No factory that valued its business would choose the former.

Even when they had no outstanding orders, the factories worked around the clock developing new weapons to pitch to the army. The cannon he'd found in the cave was likely one of those. Yet if you make weapons, there will always be people who try to take them. Tild's village had been relocated for that very reason, to avoid unfriendly eyes.

"No matter how many times we move, word always gets around. Men from other factories come snooping, some even with guns. So I have to spend all my time protecting this place, and the other kids hate me for it. Everyone hates me, and I hate them."

Roy heard not only anger toward the military in the boy's words, but anger toward the parents who had put him and the other kids in this situation.

"Even your own parents?"

"Especially them."

Tild turned away, gritting his teeth. "My dad used to dream of building a big ship and sailing around the world. But now he's using all his know-how to give the people with guns more guns, more ways to kill people! Once, when I visited the factory, I saw the head man and my father shaking hands with a military inspector. Shaking hands! How could he even look him in the face after everything the military has done to us? He didn't just sell his skill; he sold his soul, too."

Roy was silent.

"I'm through with it. The parents asked me to watch the town, and that's what I did, but no more. Not to protect something like that—a weapon that will just ruin more lives."

To Tild, the cannon was like a cross he had to bear, and

he looked ready to throw it aside. But Roy knew the power of a weapon like that, the product of so many great minds working together. It could strike a target several miles away, even knock down aerial targets. You can't keep something like that hidden for long. People would come after it sooner or later—people who would want the weapon for themselves or to sell it to the highest bidder without regard for whom that might be.

Keeping this secret exhausted Tild. It drained him of the energy to pursue his own shipwright studies and kept his attention from Zaj and the other kids who so clearly resented his distance.

Roy looked at the boy for a while before quietly asking, "Why do you think your parents hid that weapon—your parents who sold even their souls?"

"How should I know?" Tild turned away.

Roy grabbed him by the shoulder. "No, think about it. I agree with you—weapons are terrible things. If that cannon were completed, it would be incredibly powerful. That's why they've tried to hide it, don't you think?"

Tild didn't reply.

"Some weapons can be used to protect, to defend, but that weapon can be used only to destroy. If word got out about it, it would only speed up the pace of arms development, and in the end, a lot of people would die. That's why your parents have kept it hidden from the world. That's why it's here and not in the hands of some arms dealer. Can you still say they sold their souls? You still believe in your parents, somewhere in your heart, don't you? That's why you watched over the weapon for so long."

He had been on the verge of leaving town without a word, but now that Roy knew what was going on, he felt he needed to set the boy straight about his parents. He wasn't trying to ease the boy's anger. He just wanted to give meaning to what Tild had been doing for so long.

Tild thrust Roy's arm aside and slammed his fist into the wall. "What do you know?! You don't know how it feels to have everyone hate you, to do what you're told all the time! Every time Zaj or one of the others says something, it hurts. It really hurts. But I'm the oldest, so they push everything on me . . . that's why I hate grown-ups!"

Tild reached out, grabbing the handle to a drawer in a nearby cabinet. "This is what you came here for, isn't it? Here! Take it!"

Tild yanked the drawer completely out and turned it upside down. Pens, scissors, and a box of paperclips fell out onto the floor. Tild kicked at them with his foot, uncovering a single piece of paper. He picked it up and thrust it at Roy.

The paper detailed the design for the completed cannon.

"Why even try to protect something like this? What's the point?" Tild shouted. A heavy pounding came from the door.

"Tild! Tild! You there?! Open up!"

"Roy! Are you in there? We got a problem!"

Rose and Hughes were shouting outside. Roy hurriedly stuffed the designs into his pocket and opened the door. "What's going on?"

Rose craned her neck to look over Roy's shoulder at Tild standing at the back of the room. She frowned for a moment, then the tension returned to her face. "Some men have come to the village—scary men! Zaj ran into them by the field on the edge of town, and they attacked him and yelled at him. They demanded that he show them what we had hidden here. What's he talking about?!"

"Uh-oh!"

Roy grimaced. While Tild had been away from his post, men had come to the village, and he knew what they were after.

He looked down the steps to see Armstrong carrying Zaj in his arms. The boy was crying. An ugly red welt rose on his cheek. Whomever these men were, they didn't think twice about harming children, and they were definitely here for the weapons.

"Everyone's so frightened! What should we do, Tild?" Rose was shaking, still in shock from seeing Zaj getting punched.

But Tild stood with his back to the door and said nothing, a look of weary pain on his face.

"Roy," Hughes whispered. "I only saw them from a distance, but I'm sure one of the men is from that factory that tipped us off."

"You think they came here to get evidence to take to the military for themselves?"

If it became known that their competitor concealed weapons from the army, their competitor's contract would be nullified on the spot, opening the door for them.

Armstrong looked deflated. "I didn't want to leave those ruffians out there to their own means, but myself and the lieutenant colonel here had our hands full just getting Rose and the other kids to safety. And we were concerned about being found out."

Though they had only been helping out the children, these children's parents worked at factories with military contracts. It wouldn't do for high-ranking members of the military to be seen having any connection beyond pure business with people at the factory.

Roy nodded. "Understood. Leave this to me. You and Hughes can watch the children." He turned and grabbed Tild by the arm. "Let's go!"

"What are you talking about? I told you, I'm through with . . ."

"Just come on!"

Dragging the unwilling Tild behind him, Roy made for the entrance to the village. There he found them, three shady individuals standing in the clearing before the livestock pens.

"Them again," Tild muttered from behind Roy. Apparently, Tild had run into this crowd before. When they saw the boy, they laughed uproariously.

"Hey, it's you. Thought you were gone when nobody shot at us."

"Who's that? You hire a bodyguard?"

The man looked suspiciously at Roy.

"He's not my . . ." Tild began, but Roy cut him off.

"That's right. They hired me to keep trouble like you out of town."

"We did not!" Tild shouted. The three men were laughing out loud.

"You talk big for someone without any weapons," one of the men said, raising the rifle in his hands and taking casual aim on Roy. "Sorry to tell you this, but we're hired guns ourselves. I'm a pretty good shot, you know." The man's steady grip on the weapon suggested he knew what he was doing with it. "Out of the way. We came here to talk to the boy, not you."

Tild stepped forward, pushing Roy back in the direction of the village. "They don't care that you're not armed! They'll beat a scrawny guy like you down in a minute. We should just give them the plans . . ."

What could a guy who could barely wash dishes do against this lot? He reached for Roy's chest pocket. But Roy caught his hand before he pulled out the plans.

"I feel sorry for them."

"Huh?!"

Tild wasn't the only one who raised an eyebrow at Roy's swaggering confidence.

One of the men's jaws twitched. "You talk big, stranger!"

"We'll just take him and the boy out."

"I like the sound of that!"

The two men without guns raised their fists and moved in.

Roy grabbed the arm of the man going for his chest. With a quick flick of his hands, he twisted the man's wrist upward, forcing him off his feet and onto to the ground.

Next to him, Tild dodged a blow from the other man, ducking to the side, but the third man was waiting for him. "Give it up! Without your gun, you're just another scrawny brat!"

Tild jerked his head back, seeing a meaty fist swinging toward his cheek. It was too late. He closed his eyes. But the man's fist never connected.

"Huh?"

Tild opened his eyes to see Roy gripping the man's fist between his fingers. He had stopped the blow in midair!

"Tild," Roy called out, straining from the effort of holding the larger man back. "Maybe you can fight these guys off, but what about the other kids? Leave them to fend for themselves, and you're practically letting guys like this walk into town."

Tild looked down, remembering the red welt on Zaj's cheek.

"You still want to quit?" Roy asked.

"Quit? Quit what?"

"Quit protecting this village!"

Roy suddenly yanked the man's fist toward him, catching him in the stomach with his knee as he stumbled forward. The man fell moaning to the ground. Above him, Roy stood up, acting like a shield in front of Tild, facing the man with the rifle.

"Run away now, and you're running from all you've done to this day," he said to the boy over his shoulder. "Even when they hated you for it, even when they didn't understand, you still stayed on, watching over them, right?"

"I'm just saying I don't care about that stupid weapon anymore!"

"No, you weren't protecting the weapon, Tild. You were— you *are*—protecting the children! It's the most important thing you could possibly do, and with no adults around, you're the only one that can do it. You should be proud!"

Tild stared as Roy's fist caught the man on the side of his head.

The words that Tild's parents had left him with echoed in his mind.

Every time they got ready to leave the village to work, they reminded him again and again to protect the weapons. But on the day that they actually left, they never mentioned the weapon at all. They just said "take care of everyone for us."

And, he had, now that he thought about it. Whenever the kids got lonely or there was a problem, they'd always come to him. He was tired of the secrets, and the children's scorn hurt him, but now and then he did feel proud to have so many people relying on him.

He's right. I'm protecting the children.

Tild looked up and saw the man Roy had thrown to the ground stand shakily and begin to run. Tild chased after him.

"Tild! Don't go too far!"

Tild looked over his shoulder. "They're running for reinforcements! There's always a bunch hiding nearby! If I don't stop them now, the children will be in even more danger!"

Tild ran, his sense of duty pressing him even faster, and Roy followed. He couldn't run through the fields as quickly as the boy, whose agile feet knew every clump of grass and soggy mud hole in the field. By the time he reached the boulder in the woods, Tild was already positioned on top of it, his rifle raised.

"Just like I thought—they brought friends. More of them than usual."

Tild crouched, looting his rifle. He pointed downward. Roy could see no fewer than ten rough-looking men coming up the narrow, winding mountain path.

"I fire blanks just to scare them off . . . but I'm not sure how much longer that will work."

"You don't have any real rounds?"

"I do, I just don't like using them. So far, the warning shots have been enough."

This time, however, he faced more men than before, and with them so close, they might realize he was firing blanks.

"Maybe I don't have a choice," Tild muttered, clutching a box of live ammunition. His internal struggle showed on his face. Half of him didn't want to use the real bullets at any cost, and the other half grew increasingly determined to protect the village, regardless of the price.

Roy looked up at Tild with a smile, then reached out to put a hand on the boy's firing arm.

"Want me to help?"

"But there's so many of them!"

Even with Roy's impressive display of fighting techniques, he found it hard to shake the boy's image of him as useless. Even now the boy's doubtful glare made him wince.

"I may not look like much, kid, but I've got what it takes."

"Oh, yeah?"

Roy reached into his pocket and took out his glove and put it on under Tild's watchful eyes.

"Check this out," Roy said with a grin, standing up on the boulder next to the boy.

"Come no farther!" he shouted down to the climbing men. The bandits stopped in their tracks and looked up at him.

Even now in the middle of the day, the light was dim beneath the branches of the forest. The men looked up to the silhouetted form on top of the boulder. A single ray of sunlight seemed to cut through the trees above him, illuminating him so that the bandits had to squint their eyes to see him extending his arms in their direction.

The next instant, a sharp crack echoed through the woods.

"Whoa!" Tild gasped. A small flame had appeared above Roy's gloved hand. "What's that?!"

"Alchemy. I'm much better at it than housework." Roy grinned as he turned and let loose at the bandits. In an instant, the tiny flickering flame at his fingertips expanded, then split in the air, becoming several balls of fire. Each of the burning spheres glowed with a reddish light, shooting through the woods to rain down on the bandit's heads, or fall to the ground and slither on the ground toward them like snakes. The man screamed, seeing the living flame coming for them.

"You're not welcome in this village. Remember that!" Roy shouted at the backs of the fleeing man.

A minute later, all of the men were out of sight. Tild was left staring at Roy.

"I had no idea you could . . . Who are you?"

It had taken a brave stand against terrible odds—and a bit of alchemy—to do it, but finally it seemed the boy's opinion of him had changed. Tild stared at Roy's hands in amazement. "And here I thought you were useless . . ."

Tild swallowed. Not only had this man straightened out his thinking about his obligations to the village, he had just saved them all, single-handedly.

Roy shrugged. "Don't worry about it. I'm not the sort of guy you'd like anyway."

Tild raised an eyebrow. Roy handed him a small sheet of paper.

"What's this?" It was a page from a memo pad. Tild read the words on it.

"Eastern Command?"

"That's right. I'm with the military, your sworn enemy. I didn't intend to deceive you, but things just turned out that way . . . Listen, if you ever need help, you call this number here. We'll come."

On the paper was written the telephone number for the officers' room at Eastern Command, along with Roy's personal calling code.

"You're military?" Tild muttered, his eyes wide with amazement. "So wait, were you lying about dropping your money, too?"

"No, that was the truth. I dropped a good 57,000 sens in that stupid ravine."

Tild chuckled despite himself.

Then he heard the sound of children from the village.

"Tild!"

"Tild! Roy!"

The two turned in the direction of the voice, and saw Rose, Luido, Hughes, and the rest standing at the edge of the forest, peering through the trees toward them.

"Tild, where are you?"

"Are you okay, Roy?"

"They're fine, they're fine, I see both of them."

Hughes smiled at the children. Next to him, Armstrong was holding Zaj in his arms.

Roy waved, when he heard Tild whisper beside him. "Are you going to tell our secret to the military?"

He wasn't accusing. He was just making sure, wondering if he would have to move the village again. But Roy had no intention of doing anything of the sort. He knew their parents weren't the types to sell the weapon to anyone shady, and he didn't want to disturb the peaceful lives of the children living here. "Not a chance. Oh, and this is yours too," Roy said, pulling another piece of paper out of his pocket and placing it square on the boy's head. "I don't need any extra baggage on my trip down the mountain."

Tild looked up at the plans and took them, smiling.

TILD SAT ALONE on top of the boulder, looking down the mountain path. The sun was high in the sky. Far below him he could see Roy and the two other men heading down the mountain. He watched them as they dwindled into the distance.

He held the plans tightly in his hand.

When he looked up again, the three men had started to disappear over a rise in the path. Tild stood straight in the sunlight that came streaming through the branches above him. They were so far that even if they turned, they wouldn't be able to see him. He would be lost in the distance, and the light coming down on the boulder. As they passed out of view, Tild raised a hand to his forehead, the fingers straight in a salute.

Tild stood a while after he could no longer see them, then, turning around, he went to jump down and make his way back to the village. Then he noticed for the first time a small figure standing in the shadow of the rock.

"What are you doing out here, Zaj?"

Zaj stood ramrod straight, giving a formal salute. "Just copying you."

Tild's face blushed bright red. "H-hey, I wasn't . . . I was just shading my eyes from the sun!"

Before the angry Tild could grab him, Zaj bolted for the village, shouting "I know what I saw!" over his shoulder.

"Hey!" Tild laughed and chased the younger boy back across the fields.

He would go back to doing what he always had, watching over the children until their parents came back. He wasn't certain everything would go well. There would probably be more fights, more harsh words.

But now he knew that was the way it should be. The way it had to be, if he intended to keep the village safe. Tild looked at the cluster of houses standing between those well kept fields, and he felt a bit more pride than he had the day before.

"HUH, so that's what was going on."

"I finally understand what Tild was up to. Boy, that kid wasn't making any sense for a while there."

Roy explained the situation in the village to Hughes and Armstrong as they walked the gently sloping path down the mountain—a stark contrast to their vertical ascent two days before.

"Sorry, guys . . ."

The whole reason Roy and Hughes had come out here in the first place was to find that hidden weapon, and Roy knew it. Now, he had single-handedly ensured the failure of their mission. Even though they didn't seem to be outright angry with him, he felt he owed them an explanation. Still, he had expected a bigger reaction than the one he got.

"You aren't surprised at all?" Roy asked, a little deflated.

"Nah, I figured it was something like that," Hughes replied with his usual nonchalant demeanor.

"What? Don't tell me you knew they had the weapon!" They walked single file down a narrow section of the path. Roy looked back over his shoulder at Hughes.

"Well, of course we knew. Remember, we came here specifically to investigate that weapon, after all," Hughes said matter-of-factly.

Roy stopped, letting the words sink in. They didn't. "Huh?"

Hughes shook his head. "See, when we started asking questions around that abandoned village, we got solid leads suggesting that something was up near the summit of the mountain."

"You planned to come here all along?! Wait, you lied to me!"

"Nobody lied. Didn't we tell the soldiers from your base we were on a mission?"

If looks could kill, Roy's would have blasted Hughes clear across the mountainside, with Hughes chuckling all the way. Roy thought back to when he first encountered the two down at the base. When he had asked them how their investigation went, they had never told him it was over; they merely said they had gone to the wrong place.

To cover up their hiking trip, they had told those soldiers

they were going on a secret mission. Or at least Roy had assumed it was a cover.

When the rope bridge broke, they had urged Roy onward, warning that the trip might take several days to "account for uncertainties."

They had intended to investigate this village all along.

It wasn't a lie. It was worse.

Roy glared needles at Hughes.

Armstrong tried to apologize. "I'm sorry, Colonel."

"No, forget it." Roy knew who was really behind this deception, and he didn't want to give him the satisfaction of showing how much it stung.

"That's right, there's nothing to apologize for, right, Roy?" Hughes said, grinning mischievously.

"You've got plenty to apologize for!" Roy barked. They walked a little farther before Roy turned to the two once again. "Are you going to tell the military?"

Roy had promised Tild they wouldn't tell anyone, but he hadn't thought about Hughes and Armstrong or their mission. In reality, it was their jurisdiction.

Hughes waved his hand dismissively. "Wouldn't dream of it. We don't have the plans, and the cannon itself is in pieces, anyway. And I wouldn't want to tear apart those kids' houses and that windmill just to seize the remaining parts, either."

"Houses? Oh . . ."

It was at that moment that Roy finally realized that the village had another secret.

Many of those distinctively built houses along the street had sheets of metal for their roofs and windowsills. According to Armstrong, the inside of the windmill had been constructed from a part of the cannon barrel itself. The parents had scattered parts of the weapon all around town.

Hughes and Armstrong noticed that the moment they arrived. It proved better than anything that the parents of the town had no plans to sell the weapon. When they saw how much the parents treasured their own children, Hughes and Armstrong called off the investigation and instead focused on enjoying their time in the village.

"You could have said something," Roy muttered.

Hughes laughed brightly. "But we brought you along to give you a change of pace! It wouldn't have been fair for us to bring up work."

"What do you mean, a change of pace! You tricked me into going along with you. And I never saw this 'scenic view' you two were blathering about."

"Well, some rumors don't pan out, I guess. I was looking forward to it myself."

"You were looking forward to it? *I* was looking forward to it! Here, I thought we'd enjoy a nice relaxing hike, and . . ." Roy paused to catch his breath before launching into another tirade of complaints when Hughes hushed him.

"Quiet, they'll hear!" He was looking down across the mountainside. Roy followed his eyes.

They had come very close to the bottom. On the path just ahead of them stood some men in military uniforms.

"Colonel!"

"You made it!"

The soldiers ran up the path, with sergeants Natts and Cayt in the lead.

"Colonel! You won't believe what we did! While you were away, I completed the entire emergency training! Here's the report! Did we get it right?"

"I recorded every transmission," the communications officer boasted next to him. "But I keep losing all of the papers I use to record them! How do I stop that from happening, Colonel?!"

The men clustered around Roy, waving documents and books in their hands, filling the air with their reports and repeated questions. In all, nearly thirty soldiers had come to greet them. Though he certainly couldn't complain of a lukewarm welcome, only a few had really needed to come, not an entire cavalcade.

Roy, on the verge of shouting, instead took a deep breath. "Try not to leave your posts when you can avoid it," he gently reprimanded them.

Rose's words rang in his mind. *If you don't know how to do something, I'll just teach you.*

Roy felt it was egotistical of him to assume something easy for him would be easy for another.

Some people simply didn't know how to do certain tasks.

He just had to teach them—over and over if need be. After experiencing Rose's kindness as she dealt with his own ineptitude, Roy hoped he understood how his men felt a little better.

"Hey, Hughes," Roy said, tapping Hughes on the shoulder.

"Huh?"

Regardless of how it had happened, Hughes had succeeded in dragging the weary Roy away from his work at the base, and, in the end, Roy had gained something from it.

Roy smiled. "You know, it wasn't such a bad vacation after all."

TWO WEEKS LATER, when he returned to his old, familiar post at Eastern Command, Roy intended to treat his old subordinates with the same kindness he had learned to show the men at his training post.

"You've got to be nice to people, when you think about it," Roy said, smiling to himself.

No longer under the constant fear of being yelled at, the soldiers, under his training, had made incredible strides, and he had taught them things they didn't know, sometimes getting the lessons over and over until they had it down perfectly.

On the last day of his training, the men had sent Roy off with tears in their eyes, and even Roy was moved. Though his kindness might not have matched Rose's own, he felt proud that he had made it through the rest of his training without getting irritated once.

"Getting all tense and frustrated when you're busy doesn't

help a thing. You have to keep your calm, even when there's a storm around you," Roy muttered to himself as he walked down the hall at Eastern Command. He felt enlightened. The first enlisted man he ran into was Breda.

"Hey there, Colonel, welcome back!"

"It's good to be back."

"And your timing is impeccable. Could you sign these for me?"

Breda passed the stack of thick volumes of files into Roy's arms. There were twenty in all.

"Of course."

Gently. Roy smiled to himself and headed toward the officers' room carrying the files in his hands.

Falman and Fuery ran up from behind him before he reached the door. "Colonel, you're back from training! Sorry about this, but can you look over these reports before the end of the day?"

"Welcome back, Colonel. I'm gonna need you to do this for me too, would you?"

With a great fluttering of papers, roughly fifty sheets of surveys and reports joined the pile in Roy's arms.

". . . Right."

Gently. Still smiling, Roy walked into the officers' room, carrying his twenty files and fifty reports.

He walked into his office, surprising Havoc, who was in the process of adding a few more papers to the mountain already on his desk.

"Oh! Welcome back, Colonel."

"Good to see you."

"You couldn't have picked a better time to come back, sir. I was running out of places to stack these papers. Think you can get to those by tomorrow?" Havoc pointed toward a stack of cardboard boxes in the corner of the room.

"Huh?" Roy tried to put on a gentle smile, when a wrinkle formed between his eyebrows. "I can't do all that!"

It was one thing to not expect the impossible of others, but what if others expected the impossible of you? Roy grabbed Havoc's arm as the other man tried to leave the room.

"Second Lieutenant Havoc, you've got to help me."

"No way, sir."

With those three words, Havoc bolted out the door.

When someone couldn't do something, you had to teach them, to help them. Roy began to remember why he couldn't stand Eastern Command. Here, even when you couldn't do something, people just looked the other way, all the while pushing you harder and harder.

Roy sat steaming in silence, when the door opened behind him again. It was Hawkeye.

"Welcome back, Colonel."

". . . Good to be here," he mumbled.

"You hid the documents you were supposed to finish in your desk drawer before going on your training, yes? Please finish those by the end of the day. That will be all."

She hadn't added anything to the tremendous stack already

Afterword

HELLO, Makoto Inoue here.

I hope you enjoyed my little foray into the world of Hiromu Arakawa-sensei's *Fullmetal Alchemist*. The stories this time centered around little vignettes of Edward, Roy, and friends away from work, and the hardships of their journey. I hope you had fun reading them, and if parts made you chuckle, that's all the better.

This book brings the total of *Fullmetal* novels to four. I have to tell you, it's a pleasure to spend my work day immersed in the *Fullmetal* world, both as an author and as a fan of the original series.

I like it so much that I forget to leave the *Fullmetal* world when I'm not working. I'll find myself walking down the street muttering "Go, Edward, go!" or "Alphonse, no!" as I imagine various scenes playing out in my head. Before I know it, the real world has gone and passed me by.

Winter ends, spring comes and goes, summer fades away,

and . . . what? It's fall already? That's strange. I wanted to make snow angels in the winter, go see the cherry blossoms during the springtime, and what happened to my plans to go to the beach this summer? It can't be fall! What happened the rest of the year?

I know what happened. I was having fun in my own little *Fullmetal* world while my planned trips and scheduled events slipped by unnoticed. I'm sure spring was only barely beginning just the other day! Wait, if I use my imagination and squint my eyes just so . . .

Hey! Look, the cherry blossoms are blooming! It's still spring! I can go cherry-blossom viewing just like I planned! Ha ha, there's nothing better than spring in Japan. Look, the cherry blossoms are falling, just like snow. Ah ha ha ha ha ha. Ah ha ha ha ha . . .

I'm not crazy, really. I know it's September already. I know it's autumn. So what if I were the only one who could see the cherry blossoms falling? It's better than admitting the reality that the better part of a year has passed me by.

That's why I imagine . . . No, let's be frank, I fantasized that it was summer, and you know what, it's not so bad. I can fantasize with the best of them. I've had lots of practice living in my *Fullmetal* world, believe me.

So, summer is on its way. I'm definitely going to the beach soon. And I'm definitely buying myself a pair of yellow beach sandals.

So, if you see someone out on a chilly September day floating in an inner tube on the sea, it might just be me. If you see me, though, let me be. Don't call out "Are you okay?" No one knows how crazy I am better than I do, after all [*sob*].

Leaving that lonely (and, frankly, pitiful) story behind, I'd like to talk a bit about my pet. He's a chipmunk. If you don't like stories about other people's pets, sorry in advance.

So, I'm keeping this chipmunk as a pet. For those who don't know what a chipmunk is, it's a small, furry animal with brown and black stripes on its back, small enough to fit in the palm of your hand. To be honest, he's so cute, I get all googly-eyed just thinking about him.

In the wild, chipmunks carry seeds and nuts and the like in their cheeks and then bury them in the dirt or hide them beneath fallen leaves for later, and even as pets, they keep right on doing this.

Though my chipmunk usually spends most of his time in a cage, I let him out to play in the room for about an hour each day. At first, he follows me around or jumps up on my leg and is generally adorable. After a while, he tires of me, then he goes around the little room finding seeds I've placed in strategic locations. He stores them in his cheeks and zips about, finding new hiding places for his treasure trove.

I often find myself reaching in my pocket to pull out my wallet, only to discover a clump of seats instead. Or I'll be asleep and feel something tickling my feet, only to find that, after I've jumped up screaming "spider!" and generally made a fool of myself, it was just a pile of seeds in the bed. When I take a book off one of the top shelves, it's likely to come with a shower of grains and assorted nuts. My life is basically one encounter after another with seeds.

This practice, however, has led to problems. You see, seeds aren't the only thing my chipmunk hides.

Chipmunks need a lot of protein, and so in addition to seeds, I feed him mealworms—little bugs that look like tiny worms (Sorry, mealworms!). My chipmunk seems to love them . . . and you'd hope that he would eat things like vegetables and worms quickly, but that doesn't seem to be the case.

I've lifted up the carpet sometimes to see little mealworms sticking their heads out and squirming around. When I moved a piece of furniture, I found molted mealworm skins. And not just one or two, either. This happens even though I don't let him out of the cage for at least three hours after I've given him mealworms to eat.

So what, he was carrying them alive in his cheeks the whole time? Or is he hiding them in the cage for a while and then carrying them out when I open the door?

Either way, this hiding-insects-around-the-house thing has got to stop. No one wants to wake up with mealworms tucked between his toes!

Anyway, that's my pet. Cute and thrilling.

I'd like to thank Arakawa-sensei, editor Nomoto-san, and

countless other people for their help while writing this book. Thank you all so much!

Thanks also to you, the reader, for picking this book up in the first place. And thanks to everyone who's written letters. I read them all, each one carefully. It's the best part of my day!

With the greatest thanks to everybody . . . until next time.

— MAKOTO INOUE

*The following story took place just before the release of the September 2004 issue of Monthly Boys Gangan magazine.

WOOO HOOO

Editor Shimamura-san

Book Editor Nomura-san

Inoue-sensei

...At a meeting to kick off volume 4 of the novels.

And one of 'em's gonna be about Havoc.

Hic—

So, I'm thinking it'll be two stories in one.

...

Hiromu Arakawa
2004.10月つ

Inoue-sensei: Worst Timing in the World

KRAK

AGAIN!!

Check out the Gangan manga if you don't get it!

*See afterword to Fullmetal Alchemist Novel 1

AFTER-WORD

No sooner had I picked up my pen and begun to ask myself what I was going to write here than I realized I had no idea what one writes for an afterword. Let me just say that Inoue-sensei has the WORST timing of anyone on the planet (see manga for details). Hey, great job on the book, though. Whew...

2004.10

…マフィア…??